TWENTY FIRST

CENTURY AMERICAN

FAIRY TALES

B. Craig Grafton

Scarlet Leaf

2021

PUBLISHED BY SCARLET LEAF
Toronto, Canada

Table of Contents

Chapter One - Betsy Bovine

Professor Chelsea Hillary was a full professor of ancient American literature, specifically early twenty first century fairy tale literature. She had done a considerable amount of and was still doing ongoing research on this her personal topic of interest and held a doctorate in it. Now she was about to teach a postgraduate course entitled 'The Political, Historical, and Legal Ramifications of the Fairy Tales of Early Twenty First Century America and How They Relate to and Contribute to The American Culture and Society of Today. Today being the year 2525 in which mankind was still alive. It was a long name for a course simply known as American Political Fairy Tales. So as this new semester began this fine crisp autumn afternoon, she instructed her new students that at each class she would assign them homework of a couple of fairy tales to read centered on a certain theme. Then at the next couple of classes they would discuss the literary merits of these stories in detail as to symbolism, universal truths about mankind, obscure hidden meanings etc. etc. You know things like that which a writer always puts in his story to make himself look like a literary genius. And then when the discussion of those stories had run its course, she would assign a couple more stories to read and discuss again. The first of such tales she gave them to read were entitled, Betsy Bovine, The Trial of Mr. Available, The Trial of Monsieur Pierre Personne and Transgender Justice. The names of the authors of these tales and all the other tales to follow were unknown having been lost to the eons of time. The class began with Betsy Bovine.

Betsy Bovine was a milk cow. Her best friend was Peggy Porker, a sow. One day in the barnyard, during girl talk, Betsy asked Peggy, "Do you ever wish that you were a male of your species instead of a female?"

"Why heavens no. Whatever makes you ask that Betsy dear?" responded Peggy, shocked by such a question.

"Well, I read on the internet the other day this story about a male animal, a human being male animal actually, who became a human being female animal, because he believed that his mind was geared and wired toward the feminine side of things and not the masculine. So, he had a sex change operation and became a female."

"Fascinating," was Peggy's Vulcan like reply as she took another drag of her cigarette that she held ever so daintily in her hoof and then giggled, "Veeeery interesting."

"Well, what do you think?" begged Betsy.

"Think about what dear?" Peggy was nonplussed.

"If I should get the operation or not. Sometimes I feel my masculine side emerging."

"You mean you have a split personality like Dr. Jackal and Mr. Hide?"

"No not like that. More like Cat Lynn the man woman in the article."

"I say go for it, sweetie, if that's what you're sure you want to do," encouraged Peggy. "After all it's either that or a lifetime of being milked and bred. That is of course unless you don't mind those cold clamps on your udders each morning and then being put out to pasture every so often so old Mr. Avail A. Bull can jump your bones and knock you up."

"You know now that you put it that way, I'm going to do it," said a now enthused Betsy. "Males do have all the fun, don't they? They just eat and breed and leave us females alone with the hard job of raising their offspring. They got it made. Besides I don't believe that I'm cut out for motherhood anyway. By God I'm going to do it," she mooed feeling proud and assertive just like a male of her species would feel she thought.

"Well, gotta go now dearie. I've got ten hungry piglets waiting on me for their dinner." Peggy Porker stuffed out her cigarette, actually it was ditch weed rolled up in corn husks, gulped down the last of her homemade corn liquor swill and waddled her two hundred pound plus carcass back toward the farrowing house giving Betsy a rear end view of her waving her pig tail goodbye. Not a pleasant sight.

Betsy had read that Cat Lynn's surgery had been performed by one Dr. Ivanstein Muscovy. So, she made an appointment to talk to him about such an operation for herself. Dr. Muscovy was one of the few doctors in the world that performed these operations and sometimes not so successfully.

Dr. Muscovy lived in the USA now. Years ago, he had fled his homeland during the war and had been given asylum here because he was quite knowledgeable in certain scientific experimental research. But even here he was still fearful for his life because his wartime experiments had not been quite kosher. So, he tried to change his looks, he had already changed his name, by doing plastic surgery on himself. He botched the operation and left himself with a puffy, red, scarred up, bumpy face. The man was a quack.

All this was unknown to Betsy of course as she entered his office and was greeted by the doctor's bug-eyed assistant Igor Equine. She was taken back by the horrible painfully looking hump on the poor old horse's back as he sidled up to her and greeted her with a gummy hideous toothless smile. Poor Igor had previously had a terrible swayback having been ridden for many years by a three-hundred-pound female human. Dr. Muscovy had operated on him to correct the problem but unfortunately had over corrected it so that now Igor was often mistaken for a camel.

"The good doctor will see you now," he whinnied. "Walk this way please."

Betsy started to follow him when Igor suddenly turned around and scolded her. "Not like that. Like this. Like I walk." He then showed her how to walk all bent over and hobbling with the right hoof dragging the floor. Betsy imitated his walk, best she could that is, and followed him to the good doctor's office.

Dr. Muscovy with a monocle over his right eye, a scrunched-up face, and a cigarette in a long black cigarette holder dangling from his bill greeted her with a false warmness. "Willkommen, meine fraulein, you've come to the right place." Betsy was obviously a Holstein, a German breed of cow, and Dr. Muscovy therefore put a little German in his conversation to impress her and put her at ease. Though on occasion, like this time, he unconsciously still spoke in his native tongue.

"Well, I'm not quite sure that I'm ready to do this," Betsy mooed somewhat shyly.

"There's nothing to fear my dear. It's a quite safe operation and everybody is doing it nowadays. It's the in thing to do. It's trendy, fashionable. You might even say that it's chick. I mean chic. All the hep cats are doing it," he added.

Worried about what all this would cost her Betsy asked him, "Is this covered under the Affordable Animal Health Care Act?

"Not yet but the Democats are working on it and President Opossum has promised us that it will be, and he always gets his way you know."

"Well until that happens, how much will it cost me?" asked Betsy.

Dr. Muscovy told her how many clams it would set her back.

"Wow that's not chicken feed," exclaimed Betsy, taken back by the price. "I'm not sure I can afford to be a male, not just yet anyway."

"Look," said Dr. Muscovy, not wanting to lose a sale. "Tell you what I'll do. I'll give you, at the same cost, an operation that still leaves you as a female but adds the male organs. That way you can try it out and if you don't like it, you can go back to the way you were. There will be no charge for the reverse operation. Furthermore, at no charge to you also, I'll convert you to all male of the species if that's what you want. Or you can remain dual gender and have the best of both worlds."

"Dual gender?" asked Betsy.

"Oh yes, dual gender. It's the next big thing. Pretty soon every animal in the world will be wanting to be dual gendered. Just you wait and see. And you my dear can be at the forefront of it all just like Cat Lynn was with her operation." Dr. Muscovy had never done a dual gender operation. But what the heck he thought. If he could pull that off, he would make a lot of money and acquire a nice little nest egg to retire on.

"I need to go back to the farm and think about all this," said Betsy as politely as she could, still in sticker shock.

"Okay then," replied Dr. Muscovy, realizing that he hadn't made a sale today but not willing to give up just yet. So, the sales pitched, "But don't take too long. Our dual gender offer is a limited time offer only. Act now and save."

Betsy went back to the barnyard and talked to Peggy about all this.

"Sounds like a bargain to me Betsy dearie. You can have the best of both worlds."

"What about the worst of both worlds Peggy. I don't want to be fixed with that."

"Just have the doctor reverse you back then. Besides, it might be a hoot being male and female at the same time. Sorry dearie but I've gotta go now. My break is over." she said, stuffing the last of her pork rinds in her mouth. "Got nine hungry piglets wanting on me for supper."

"I thought you had ten."

"I did but last night in my sleep I rolled over on one and crushed him, or her, to death. Got nine now."

"Oh, I'm sorry," said Betsy.

"Don't be. It's no big deal. Soon as this litter of Porker piglets is shipped off to the pig parlor, I'll be making more anyway. Bye."

Betsy thought it over, decided to not to be chicken any longer and get this over with. So, she saved up her milk money, accepted the limited time offer, it was still open, and scheduled a time for the operation.

Dr. Muscovy operated and after the anesthesia wore off, he met with her for a little postoperative chat.

"The operation was a success dear, or should I say sir, or should I say dear sir," he chuckled, proud of himself for his corny humor. "Take a peek and see for yourself."

Betsy lifted her sheet and looked at her nether regions. She was now plumbed both ways.

"Now let me give you some advice before you're discharged. Since you have two sexes now, whenever you are aroused, both sets of sexual equipment will be fully functional at the same time. Therefore, before you go for that proverbial roll in the hay make sure you tell your partner that you're acting either as a male or a female. This will avoid any unnecessary embarrassment for the both of you." Dr. Muscovy tried to stifle a cackling little quack but was unable to do so.

"Thank you for that information doctor," Betsy said somewhat hesitatingly.

"Bitte," he said.

"Huh?" said Betsy, for she could not speak German even if she was of German descent.

"Igor will show you out," responded Dr. Muscovy quickly, anxious to get her out of there before she asked any questions.

"Walk this way please," said Igor again.

Betsy did not need to be cued this time as she again imitated Igor's walk until he was out of her sight.

Back at the farm Betsy went about her business of being a milk cow. She was not quite ready to act as a bull yet, but she still dreamed about being one, dreamed both daydreams and nightdreams about it. And one night while sleeping she had one of those wet dreams. Not having been a male before she was not sure what had happened. But she soon was sure about one thing. Sure that she was pregnant now. Wondering how this could have happened without having had any sexual contact with a bull, she went back to Dr. Muscovy for an explanation.

"Unfortunately, this is one of the side effects of being dual gendered, becoming self-impregnated that is. I can abort the calf if you wish at no charge to you. All abortions are free under Opossum Care," Dr. Muscovy informed her.

Betsy was now thoroughly disgusted now with this whole gender thing. "You told me that I would have the best of both worlds and what I got was the worst of both worlds," she screamed. "My lawyers Donkey, Cheetah and Cow will be getting in touch with you, you quack."

Igor did not show her out. She knew the way and the walk by now.

Back at the farm Farmer Dell noticed Betsey's pregnancy and didn't like what he saw. He had told Betsy to have the operation thinking that he would then have two bovines for the price of one. Then he could sell Mr. Avail A. Bull for hamburger, use Betsy for breeding purposes and when that was done have her go back to being a milk cow. He didn't want her inbreeding herself and producing deformed hideous looking mutated calves. No she would have to go. So next Monday morning he took her to the sale barn and she, not Mr. Avail A. Bull, became hamburger.
Moral of the story: Be cowful of what you ask for, you might not live to regret it.

So, at the next class Professor Hillary took the class through the symbolism of each character, that is what each character represented and stood for, how the author effectively used play on words, irony, historical references to American culture, and comedy and tragedy in the story. The class took copious notes for they knew at test time that they would be called upon to regurgitate everything Professor Hillary admired and liked about the story. What they personally took away from it mattered not, for only what the Professor saw in it would be what she wanted to hear on the test. This was because students were not taught, not even allowed to think for themselves. Thinking for them was part of the teacher's job description.

The second story discussed had a bovine theme to it too and it was called The Trial of Mr. Available.

Chapter Two - Trial of Mr. Available

Mr. M. Available, the M was for Manfred, was a Black Angus bull on trial for his life, i.e. his right to exist as a male of his species. He was a peaceful individual by nature and never expected to go to war with the Bovine Women's Moovement. But now they wanted to make mincemeat or rather hamburger out of him. They had accused him of numerous unmentionable sexist crimes against the humanity of women.

His attorney was Red McRooster, a red feathery old fowl of a fellow with a bright red comb that always stood upright, stayed in place, and never flopped around. Some say that wasn't natural and that he used lots of hairspray to keep it that way. His defense to all these 'trumped' up charges as he called them was the classic 'femme fatale' defense. That is females, especially the sexy sultry kind, like these accusers, were the ruination of not only his client but of men everywhere and not the other way around as they alleged.

Representing the State was Wren Deering, a flighty, fighty, flutter of feminine featherhood. She had the bulldog tenacity of a pitbull and Red knew that he was in for one tough hard cock fight.

15

The judge was The Most Honorable Judge Trudith Schweinlin commonly known as Judge Trudy and she was a self-admitted femme legalist.

They now all were engaged in the process of picking the last juror and so far the jury was diverse to say the least. It was comprised of a mixed breeds herd of Herefords, Guernseys, Holsteins, Limousins, Charlaises, Jerseys, Longhorns, and one purple cow, which no one had hoped to see and certainly no one hoped to be one. But alas not one Black Angus was on the jury nor was there one male of the species either. They were all cows. Mr. McRooster objected that having all those females on the jury was unfair and prejudicial to his client. To which Judge Trudy replied that his client was indeed getting a fair trial by a jury of his peers because peers mean equals and females and males were all equal under the law. And when he objected that there were no Black Angus on the jury, she convolutedly countered that there was already enough diversity on the jury and that too much diversity was not a good thing and in fact could be harmful to the judicial governmental system for then there would be no unity, no tying link that binds and brings us all together and gives us closure. In other words, it wasn't sustainable, she said.

Red McRooster scratched his comb on his head until it bled trying to figure that one out. But he still had one last chance though. As said one more juror needed to be picked and the prospective juror now before the court was one Stevie Steer, not a bull, a former bull, now a steer, yet still a male, kind of. Being a steer, he had been 'degenderized' and because of that Wren Deering had no objection to him being on the jury nor did Judge Trudy. In fact, Judge Trudy thought it would be cool, i.e. enlightened, to have a genderless no gender person on the jury. Red McRooster had no objection either. He would play on this former male's sympathies, harken him back to the days of his youth when he was a real man and thus bring out those sympathies to persuade him to find in favor of his client.

And so, the trial began.

Wren Deering called her first witness the Complainant one Mamie, aka, Mame Moorow. Mamie Moorow the famous bovine actress.

"Please tell us Miss Moorow when you first came to know Mr. Available, in the Biblical sense of the word that is," she asked, inquiring titillated minds wanted to know.

"Well, I was put out to pasture by the dairy/cattle industrial complex with the Defendant many, many, years ago. I can't remember exactly when and where or any dates or things like that because it was such a long, long time ago. But I'll never forget what he did to me. That's for sure." She wiped a tear from her big brown eyes.

The jury was mooved.

"And what did he do to you dear?"

"He impregnated me. That's what he did."

Gasp! Gasp!

"How many times dear?"

"I can't remember. Just many that's all."

"Your Witness Mr. McRooster," chirped Wren.

"No questions Madame Your Honor," McRooster then offered a stipulation. "In the interest of judicial efficiency the defense will stipulate that the testimony of the next dozen witnesses or so that the State intends to call will all be of the same nature as Miss Moorow's testimony and thus just be a repeat of a bunch of sad but titillating tails, excuse me tales, and a waste of the court's time. We'll accept their testimony as being the same as Miss Moorow's." He then went on and on repeating this point over and over for the next ten minutes or so until Judge Trudy finally cut him off with, "What say you, Miss Deering?"

"No objection Your Honor as long as the Defendant admits to impregnating eighty-six other females and some of them a couple of times or more."

"So agreed Your Honorness," crowed McRooster.

"We rest then Your Honor," twerped Prosecutor Deering. Such overwhelming mountains of evidence and a pro female judge was a slam dunk conviction as far as she was concerned.

"Call your first witness Mr. McRooster."

"The defense calls Peggy Porker."

"Objection Your Judgement. That woman is a pig and unfit to testify in these matters of bovines."

"Your Holiness, she is a woman and therefore qualified to speak to all things female regardless of her ethnicity."

Judge Trudith Schweinlin was proud of her swineish heritage. She wasn't going to deny one of her own the privilege of testifying in her court.

"Miss Porker may testify."

"Thank you, Your Graciousness. Miss Porker please state your name and address for the record."

"My name is Margaret Porker, but everyone calls me Peggy. I live at Dell Manor Farm rural route 1 Jonestown here in the state of Confusionia."

"And what do you do there?"

"I produce piglets."

"And are you good at your job?"

"Very,"

"And are you familiar with one with one Mamie Moorow who resides there too?"

"Yes. She's a milch cow. Know her quite well."

"And what is her job?"

"Well besides getting her udders milked daily she produces calves. You could say that she's like me in the reproduction business."

"And what would happen to her or to you too for that matter if you didn't reproduce?"

"We'd be out of a job."

"How so?"

"Like we'd become sausage or mystery meat for Spam or something like that,"

"So, is it safe to say that you and Miss Moorow are actually just doing your jobs by getting knocked up and that you are actually advancing your careers in the process by doing so?"

"Yes, that would be safe to say."

"No further questions. Your witness Miss Endearing," mocked Red McRooster.

Ms. Deering flew up to the witness stand and fluttered in Peggy's face.

"Is it also safe to say that Farmer Dell, your boss, could have just as easily had you artificially inseminated?"

"I suppose that's possible."

"And isn't it also possible that he could have had Miss Moorow artificially inseminated instead of letting the Defendant here, Mr. Available, have his way with her?"

"Oh, I suppose that's possible. But what's the fun in that dearie?"

That last remark drew a stifled chuckle from Stevie Steer. Red McRooster, saw it, picked up on it, and winked at him. Stevie gave him a thumbs up and winked back.

Then Ms. Deering made the classic lawyerly mistake of not quitting when you're behind, of asking that one question too many.

"But it is possible, isn't it?" she insisted.

"Yes, suppose it's possible if you don't mind someone sticking their arm up to their elbow in your butt and mess around with your insides for a few minutes and hope that they get it right the first time, so they don't have to do it again. Yes, that's possible."

The jury dropped their jaws. Their mouths were locked open in shock.

Wren Deering slumped down in her chair and tweeted, "No further questions." Her cross examination had been self-rendered worthless.

"Next witness Mr. Mc Rooster," grunted Judge Trudy.

"The defense calls the Defendant Mr. Manfred Available," cackled attorney McRooster.

Mr. Available humbly took the stand, head upright and proud, he raised his right hoof and was sworn in while in his left hoof he waved a miniature American flag.

"State your name and address please", squawked McRooster.

"My name is Manfred Available, and I live at the same farm as Peggy and Mamie."

"Please tell us how Miss Mamie Moorow came to know you in the Biblical sense of the word that is."

"Well like always I was put out to pasture, minding my own business, just chewing my cud, ruminating and all, when she comes up beside me and starts rubbing up against me getting me all excited and stuff if you know what I mean."

"Then what did you do?"

"What could I do? She starts batting those long eyelashes of hers at me, looking at me with those big beautiful brown eyes, and then waving those big baggy udders of hers back and forth."

That last remark got two thumbs up from Stevie Steer.

"Then she starts whining and tells me that she needs to get pregnant to keep her job and advance her career and would I help her with that."

"So, what did you do?"

"What could I do? I didn't want the poor girl to lose her job. So, I did what any gentleman would do. That's all."

"So, this wasn't your fault then, was it?

"No, it wasn't. I blame Mame. I put the blame on------on her."

"Your witness Ms. Deer Run."

"And it wasn't your fault in the other eighty-six cases either, was it Mr. Available? Was it?" she screeched.

"No, it wasn't. Can I help it if eighty-six women just happen to be in the same pasture as I'm in. I'm the one who's the victim here, not them."

With that answer both sides rested, and the case went to the jury.

Hours later the jury came back. Not guilty. Stevie Steer, being a kind of man, was the jury foreman, and he put the 'man' back into foreman and steered the jury his way.

Judge Trudy couldn't believe it. It went against the weight of the evidence on her judicial scales of justice. Being a woman, she couldn't have such an outrageousness anti-woman ruling in her court. Some had to pay. Someone had to be hung out to dry, hung out to dry like they dry cow hides that is. So, she had bailiff Bird steer the jury out of the courtroom and onto an awaiting cattle truck where the jury was cattle called and hauled to the local abattoir, that's slaughterhouse in English. Within twenty-four hour hours the jury was rendered into corned beef, beef jerky, 10 percent beef hot dogs, 10 percent beef burgers and parts of them like intestines, brains, stomachs, eyes, hooves and jaws, into Spam.

As said someone had to pay and if it wasn't going to be the defendant then by god Judge Trudy, or by God Judge Trudy, had seen to it that the jury paid for this stillborn miscarriage of justice. And as a final note to prevent this from ever happening again, no longer would the prejudicial word foreman be used in her courtroom. From now on it would be forewoman.

"This story was probably by the same author," said Professor Hillary. "And it satirized human sexual harassment. Now I know no such thing as sexual harassment exists anymore but sometimes, we need to know of these things lest we forget."

The students had a hard time grasping this content because as said it was something totally unknown and foreign to their way of thinking. But nevertheless, they took copious notes on it since Professor Hillary seemed fascinated by it as she expounded on it for some length of time.

"Next time class we will discuss another trial, The Trial of Monsieur Pierre Personne. People back then seemed to be fascinated by the legal system and you will note that trials come up quite often as the setting for these fairy Note the gender identity crisis in this story too as you read it. It was quite pervasive and perverted in society back then. See you tomorrow."

Chapter Three - The Trial of Monsieur Pierre Personne

Judge Trudith Schweinlin presided over the trial of one Monsieur Pierre Personne who was charged with failing to comply with an executive order. Judge Trudy, as she was known, was small for a schwein and must have been the runt of the litter. But her hair was perfect.

The prosecutor was Miles Mole, a little creature himself with a turned up pink nose and buck teeth. The courtroom lighting hurt his eyes so much that he wore his prescription sunglasses whenever he appeared in court.

The defense attorney Oyster Shyster was a tight-lipped individual who held his cards close to his vest and never smiled and that was a shame because he had such pearly white teeth.

And as to Monsieur Personne, the poor soul on trial here, well he viewed himself as an intellectual like his heroes Sartre and Camus. In fact, he admired them so much that when confronted with a problem he 'existentialized' it to death before deciding upon a course of action.

"Call your first witness Mr. Mole," grunted Judge Trudy.

"The Prosecution calls Officer Shepherd."

Bailiff Byrd swore in the witness.

A big fierce looking German Shepherd, Officer Shepherd took the stand.

"State your name and occupation please."

"Wolf Shepherd, police dog, K-9 unit," he barked out loud and clear.

"Officer would you please tell the court what you saw at the City Dog Park on the night in question."

"I observed a human being, later identified as the defendant, standing next to a tree, his back to me and his hands held about waist high in front of himself, relieving himself on the tree."

"And were there facilities at the park for human beings to relieve themselves, Officer?"

"Yes, the city had just built a new multi gender friendly, state of the art facility there which is in full compliance with all executive orders on genderism."

"But Monsieur Personne was using a tree instead, wasn't he? And therefore, he was not in compliance with federal law, was he?"

"Yes, that is correct. I asked him what he was doing there, and he said, and here I quote, he said, 'Relieving myself.' I then arrested him."

"No further questions Your Honor."

"Mr. Shyster, your turn," ordered Judge Trudy.

"No questions Your Honor." Oyster Shyster would have his client explain all that away later.

"Mr. Mole, any other witnesses?"

"Yes, Your Honor the prosecution calls Rusty, Monsieur Personne's dog.

Bailiff Byrd swore Rusty in.

Rusty was a French Poodle show dog. The French Poodle dog breeders had put so much emphasis on creating the perfect French Poodle specimen, and inbreed them so much so, that they had literally bred the brains out of the breed. Rusty was a prime example of this.

"State your name and what you do for a living please."

"My name is Rusty and I work for Monsieur Personne as his best friend. After all, I am a dog you know," giggled Rusty with a slight French accent.

"And on the night in question you saw him relieve himself on a tree at the dog park, didn't you?"

"No, I didn't."

"Rusty let me remind you that you've been subpoenaed here to tell the truth. So, I ask you again, what did you see Monsieur Personne do?"

"I didn't see him do anything," said Rusty, twisting his chin upward defiantly.

"Are you sure?" taunted Mr. Mole. "Weren't you at the tree next to him doing what he was doing?"

"Yes, I'm sure and yes I was at the tree next to him peeing," barked out Rusty, fidgeting in his seat. Things were starting to literally get a little hot around the collar for him now, so he stuck his paw under his collar, pulled it away from his neck, and audibly gulped.

"And you're sure you saw him do nothing."

"Absolutely!" growled Rusty.

"And why are you so sure of that Rusty?"

"Because I was too busy doing what he was doing to see anything."

"Your witness Mr. Shyster," said Mr. Mole triumphantly.

"No questions Your Honor." Oyster Shyster would have his client explain this away later too.

"Anything else Mr. Mole?" grunted Judge Trudy.

"Nothing Your Honor."

"Then the prosecution rests I take it Mr. Mole," stated Judge Trudy, not asking a question but giving him a directive, her eyebrows raised, her head nodding affirmatively up and down.

"Yes, Your Honor. The prosecution rests," answered Mr. Mole, taking the hint.

"Your turn Mr. Shyster," squealed Judge Trudy.

"The defense calls the defendant."

Bailiff Byrd swore in poor Monsieur Personne.

Monsieur Personne worked for the government gathering information on people for purposes unbeknownst to him, just a drone in a hive of continual governmental activity. But today was his chance to bee somebody and he was all abuzz about testifying.

"Monsieur Personne," began Oyster Shyster, "on the night in question did you take Rusty to the local dog park here in town?"

"Yes, I took him there so that he could socialize."

"And on this occasion did you have to relieve your bladder."

"Yes, I did."

"In your own words tell us what happened then."

"Well, I noticed that a new facility had been built there. I wasn't familiar with all the pictures on the door, men, women, kids, men in skirts. I didn't know what that all meant. There's no wording anymore, just pictures for all those dummies out there who can't read. Then Rusty tells me it's a multi-gender bathroom so humans who have gender identity problems don't become stressed out having to pick a gender specific facility. But I don't have a gender identity problem and so I came to the conclusion that I could not in good conscience choose to use this facility. My choice was for a gender specific facility. So, I walked around the park looking for one but couldn't find one. Meanwhile the pressure is building if you know what I mean. And then I see Rusty sniffing around a tree and Eureka! I have found it, found my choice. The answer was logically simple. The problem here is that we humans choose to act as humans and not as animals. But we humans, we're animals too, and animals have choices and voila if animals have choices, then us humans as animals have the same choices that they do. And one of those choices is the right to relieve oneself where one pleases. So, voila again I exercised my choice, my right." Pierre Personne held his head high aloft, smugly proud of his logic.

Oyster Shyster shuttered and continued, "When you told Office Shepherd that you were relieving yourself what did you mean by that?"

"I meant it figuratively, existentially, not literally. I meant that I was relieving myself from the restraints and regulations that we humans place on each other and invoking my animal rights choice, which is what we are after all, we're all just basically animals you know."

Mr. Mole rose from his chair, his head barely above the prosecution's table. "Objection Your Honor. Move to strike all of defendant's testimony as irrelevant and pure unadulterated hogwash."

"Hogwash Mr. Mole? Is that a wise choice of words here?" scolded Judy Trudy, a woman proud of her schwienish heritage.

"Bull then Your Honor."

"Oh, now you've done it Mr. Mole. You've managed to get both of those tiny little feet of yours in that big mouth of yours. What say you Mr. Shyster?"

Mr. Shyster had nothing to say so he clammed up. The cat was out of the bag, so to speak.

"Cat got your tongue?" snickered Judge Trudy.

Then looking down at Mr. Mole she grunted, "Mr. Mole I'm granting your motion not because it's hogwash or bull but because the defendant's testimony here is Looney

Tunes, pure, total, unadulterated Looney Tunes." She leaned over towards the defendant and shouted, "Pure Looney Tunes. You hear me Mister Monsieur. Pure Looney Tunes."

Then slumping back down into her chair, disgusted with all this jabberwocky, and in her normal grating shrill voice made her ruling. "I've heard enough. I hereby find the defendant guilty of disobeying an executive order. What sentence do you wish for me to impose Mr. Mole?"

A crinkly little smile appeared on Mr. Mole's face gloating in victory. "The law is quite clear here Your Honor. Under the Penal Code of Political Correctness when one disobeys an executive order, one is confined to a political correctness rehabilitation center until such time as one is certified to be politically correct in his thinking."

"So be it. We're done here," said Judge Trudy as she rose from the bench and hauled her carcass out of the courtroom.

Oyster Shyster pried himself from his chair as the press began badgering him with questions. But he remained tight-lipped, shucked himself rid of them and scuttled out of the courtroom.

And as to Monsieur Personne, well he had only one question as Bailiff Byrd led him away. "You think I'll have a choice of facilities there?"

"Duuuuh think about it Personne," responded Byrd. Then he paused and added, "On second thought, don't."

Again, the class was fascinated by this story. What was such a big deal they thought about having separate bathrooms anyway. That was as wrong as having separate drinking fountains for the races back in early twentieth century America.

"You can see class how far we've come," said Professor Hillary. "This story actually was what helped us get on the right track as to the disposal of our bodily functions by using the concept of equality.

Now as I pointed out there was quite the fascination with sex back then. Everything seemed to revolve around sex. So to stay on the same page so to speak, no pun intended," (There wasn't one here anyway.) "The next story for you to read is entitled 'The Monkey's Trail' and it deals with sex and marriage and how the legal system again was always the way to resolve things back then and how things were pushed to their logical legal conclusion."

They read The Monkeys' Trial as follows.

Chapter Four - The Monkeys' Trial

"The right to marry is a fundamental constitutional right Your Honor. The Supreme Court has already ruled that." Howler Monkey, the Plaintiff's attorney, smiled as he said that. He knew this case was already won. After all, the big ape himself, Judge Banga Kong, sat on the branch. Howler knew that the judge liked cases like this one, one where he could flex his judicial muscles and rule supreme over all the beings of the jungle out there.

"Objection Your Honor. The right to commit bigamy is not a fundamental right. It is a fundamental wrong against the laws of civilized people everywhere." Ben Church, a member of the highest species of the ape world, the homo sapiens, and assistant Attorney General for the State of Confusionia, spoke up knowing that he was fighting a losing battle here but felt he had to say something, something for all those conservative human beings out there who had elected his boss Attorney General.

"No one has been charged with bigamy here Mr. Church," roared Judge Kong. "This case is one of a declaratory judgement. The court has been asked here to rule whether Ms.
Cherry Chimp can be married to two husbands at the same time in the light of the Supreme Court's recent ruling."

Cherry Chimp already had one mate and was asking the court to rule if she could now have two at the same time. She didn't want to marry spouse number two and then be charged with bigamy.

"Yes, Your Honor," was attorney Church's meek response as he humbly sat down knowing his place in the pecking order.

"Continue Howler," said the judge amicably to his old friend. He and Howler had once worked together for the law firm of Monkeysee and Monkeydew.

"Thank you, Your Honor." Howler knew that he didn't have to say much, just a few words of legal liberal mumbo jumbo that the judge liked to be fed, then sit down and shut up. Church will barf up the usual right wing humanistic feedback and Judge Kong will throw it back in his face, rule against him and then we'll all go home. But not right away, that is, not until Howler had talked to the press and milked all the coconut juice that he could from this case. For after all, that's why he took it in the first place.

So, he continued, "The right to marriage is like any other right, an ongoing right. You don't just use it once and throw it away. It's reusable. No expiration date comes with it. It has no shelf life. You can exercise that right over and over just like you do when you vote in election after election. To say that it can only be used once is to make it something less than a right. It is to make it a privilege, and only the state can grant privileges and that's what the state wants to do here, wants to make your right a privilege and grant it to you only on their terms and conditions."

Howler stopped. He knew that this all sounded corny, hokey, but he didn't care, he was in too deep to back out now. His client was the one who had dreamed up this case and he knew that it was hogwash to begin with. She did it as a sale gimmick hoping to draw national attention to her boutique and line of erotic feminine apparel, Chimporia's Secrets, which was fighting to stay alive in the commercial jungle out there. Now, by filing this case, she had instant international press coverage and thanks to Mr. Al Boar and the internet was making a killing in sales.

Ms. Cherry Chimp already had a mate, one Harry Orangutang, who ran his own jungle gym business. But now she wanted to marry one Lar Gibbon, a primatologist. So according to her testimony anyway, she would have both a hunky husband and a brainy one, the best of both worlds. But everyone knew all this was just a crock, a way to jungle drum-up business. In fact, the whole village had encouraged her to do it to bring tourists to town which in fact it did. A couple of sightseeing tour businesses had already sprung up and the local motels and restaurants were packed with rubber neckers. Trade was good. Howler had known this right from the start and business was good for him too.

So, on he went. "The right to more than one mate is not just an animal thing Your Honor. The right to more than one 'spouse', as our cousins call them, is as old as their own evolution itself and has been proven throughout their own history. Father Abraham and other Biblical figures had more than one wife. And if a male can have more than one wife, then today, under equal rights, under the law of no discrimination because of one's sex, specie, or gender, then my client certainly can have more than one mate, or 'husband' as Mr. Church prefers to call them, because that right is based on their kinds own historical biblical facts."

Historical biblical facts, now there's an oxymoron for you if there ever was one, chuckled Howler to himself.

Judge Kong pointedly interrupted, "Howler this is not a matter of religion. The jungle out there is not a Christian jungle. It recognizes the rights of all religions to survive based on their own adaptations to the environment. Make your point here or drop it." Judge Kong made this comment for show only. He knew that he must appear to be fair and not show any specie bias.

"That's my point exactly here Your Honor. We must recognize the rights of all religions," responded Howler hoping to build on the lead that the Judge had just given him. "All religions are equal under the law of the jungle, and none should be denied the right to practice their own rites and rituals. But sadly, this has not always been the case in this country. For example, the first true Americans, Native Americans, under their beliefs allowed one to have more than one wife, but they are not allowed to do so today, and the Mormons likewise, they have been illegally deprived of their rights to multiple spouses also, and today even Muslims, yes Muslim Americans, are denied the right to have four wives as allowed by their religion. The court must correct all these abominations and right the ship here because what has happened in the past is against the laws of Mother Nature herself. And now you Your Honor, only you, (Judge Kong loved to be kowtowed to), can set the record straight and undo these grievous wrongs of the past. We therefore humbly ask the court to do so." Howler sat down, proud of himself. His client touched him on the shoulder in dramatic fashion making sure the press saw her thank him as she emoted her feelings before the cameras. Journalist integrity aside, they loved this kind of drama news.

"Mr. Church, your turn," grunted Judge Kong.

Ben Church rose slowly. He knew what he said would make no difference. The outcome had already been decided but he had to say something. "Your Honor, religion doesn't trump crime. It may not be a crime as to one's religion to do something but that is beside the point. If the State, the people, through their elected representatives, enact a law making it a crime, it's a crime. We cannot allow bigamy here which is a crime.

As to my opponent's ridiculous arguments, first the Bible is not the law of the land. It's a great holy script, a great moral guide but it's not a state statute and no one's claiming it is. More power to my fellow Christians out there who believe in it, but It doesn't apply here. And as to whatever the Native Americans allowed as to the number of wives also has no bearing here, maybe within their own tribal communities they can do what they want, but off the reservation state law still applies. And as to the Church of the Latter-Day Saints, well the Saints agreed to ban multiple marriages as part of their deal to be admitted to the Union as the state of Utah. Therefore, they must be held to their bargain. Mormons are honorable people and abide by their bargains. And finally, as to American Muslims, there's nothing to stop them from going to a Muslim country and being married there four times if they want. No U.S. law can prevent that. Furthermore, the courts in this country recognize all those marriages as legal. For these reasons Your Honor, you must deny Plaintiff's request. The State rests. Thank you."

With that Attorney Church sat down confident that he had not offended Christians, Native Americans, Mormons or Muslims, but taking little comfort in anything else.

"Anything further Howler?" asked Kong.

"No, Your Honor."

"Alright then I will give you my ruling tomorrow morning. Court's adjourned until then."

Judge Kong went back to his chambers. He had to rule whether it was or was not a fundamental right to marry a number of spouses at the same time. All this had illogically been brought about because of the Supreme Court's recent same sex marriage ruling. So, he began turning the legal wheels in his walnut sized brain.

As to the facts here, they were not in dispute. It was obvious to him, and to the world, that this was just another monkey trial. The Plaintiff's concern wasn't love or rights or religion. No, it was money that drove her. But all this was beside the point, a ruling had to be made even if this was an abuse of the judicial system.

"Everyone remembers Clarence Sparrow and William Jennings Lion from their monkey trial," Banga said to himself, "but no one remembers the judge's name, do they? But by God, this time they will."

If he ruled against Ms. Cherry Chimp, that would probably be the end of it. She won't want to bear the expenses of an appeal as she would already have gotten all that she wanted out of this case anyway. But if he ruled for her, the State was sure to appeal and his name would still be alive, still be in the news, maybe all the way to the Supreme Court itself. No, he'd never get another chance like this. His ruling was a foregone conclusion, and those animals out there, waiting to feed on his every word, knew it.

"As you will note class," said Professor Hillary, "there was quite the fascination with the concept of marriage back then. Thank God that too has become obsolete now. Anyway, our next story still deals with sex too for as I told you, sex was a big deal back then. This story is about a sex change operation as they called them back then. Of course, nowadays what they called sex change operations are called gender plastic surgery since no one can actually change their gender. A male becoming a female can't get pregnant and bear a child any more than a female who became male can impregnate anyone. It took a couple of centuries for this to be realized so just keep it in when you read Transgender Justice.

Chapter Five - Transgender Justice

This whole proceeding was just plain crazy thought Judge Jellico. But craziness had become the new norm and everything crazy lands up in court nowadays and this particular brand of craziness landed before him. It was a petition wherein a youth was praying for his old life back. 'His' being the key word here. The petition alleged that she, the youth that is, had been a 'he' before but when his mother saw him as a young boy, well actually he was thirteen at the time, trying on her clothes, she assumed that he really wanted to be a she and so she had him changed through surgical procedures. The mother believed that this was in the best interest of her child to do so and after getting some bad medical advice proceeded with the transformation operation. The operation cost her nothing under her insurance since such operations were encouraged and now subsidized by the federal government. Never mind that he was just being a goofy teenager when he dressed up in her clothes. She was his mother, and she knew what was best for him. So, he became Craigina. Before that he was just plain Craig. Now through his attorney, Chutney Winston Pitbull, he was asking the court to restore him to his old self. Chutney Winston Pitbull was an attorney who would take on any case, as long as there was money involved, for him that is.

At the other table sat the youth's mother Olivia. She had been born Oliver but she transgendered herself to Olivia and then adopted Craig when he was just baby as a single mom. She was proud of her status as a single mom. Proud that she was a woman defying a system that did her wrong daily and beating the odds raising a child in a man dominated society prejudiced against women. Next to her sat her attorney Jane Doe who had guaranteed her that the law would not grant her daughter's request. Guaranteed her that it is a woman's right to change the sex of her child if she so wished to do so. Just like a woman's right to an abortion. That this was just another woman's health issue she told her and that she was sure to win.

So it came to pass that Judge Evan Jellico was called to hear this case. He had first been called to the Lord as a minister, then to the bar, then to the bench and now here today he was to rule on motions on summary judgement. Both sides had filed motions for summary judgment. That is both parties alleged the other had no case, that there are no facts in dispute and therefore they were entitled to have the other's case thrown out as a matter of law without a trial.

The bailiff called the court to order and Judge Jellco began, "I have read the complaint and answer counsellors. It is my understanding that the plaintiff here wants to become a male again so that he or she can compete in male high school athletics as a male this coming spring. Is that correct Mr. Pitbull?"

Mr. Pitbull rose from his chair. He was a short stocky solid older balding man who bore the scars of many a court dog fight. Yet there was still a lot of fight left in this old dog, and he was an old dog who could and did learn new tricks, especially if they were dirty tricks.

"Yes, Your Honor," he gruffed. "My client won the state title last year in the women's one hundred- and two-hundred-yard races and now wants to become the first person in history to win the same events both as a male and as a female. This is his last year in high school. His last chance to do so, and that's why he wants to become a male again." Mr. Pitbull kind of growled when he spoke, and this irritated Attorney Doe to no end so that's why he did it.

"What say you, Miss Doe?"

"Your Honor," she said firmly, looking him disapprovingly in the eye for calling her miss. "Women's rights are at stake here. The right of a woman to raise her child as she deems in the best interests of that child is what is at stake here. It is undisputed as a matter of law that a mother decides how to raise her child, not the child. The Plaintiff has no case here." Jane Doe was a stick figure of a woman with short cut gray hair, hair cropped so close that from a distance one might mistake her for a man. Her gray flannel suit matched her hair and her rimless granny glasses perched on her cute little turned up freckled nose gave her a tomboyish look. No matter how hard she tried to look genderless her nose and face would always give her away as a woman. She had been an advocate for women's rights, gay and lesbian rights, transgender rights, and any other type of sexual oriented rights all her life except of course for the sexual rights of men. Her bright blue eyes sparkled whenever she spoke up for a cause that she believed in like they did now. Her birth name wasn't Jane Doe. She had been born something else, a name much more feminine and daintier and cuter that her parents had given her. But over the years she came to view herself as an invisible person in society, invisible because she was a woman, and thus just another Jane Doe, a nameless woman. So, she changed it, legally of course.

"Your Honor," spoke up attorney Pitbull. "What is not in dispute here is the fact that this woman," and here he pointed to Olivia, "if that's what she really is, a woman, has committed child abuse by mutilating the body of this young man. This court cannot and must not let this abuse to continue. The court must correct this misfortune, this tragedy to my client. He must be returned to the sex that God gave him." Get God involved in this thought Chutney Pitbull. This judge loves it when you do so. If you're on God's side you're on the Judge's side too.

"Mr. Pitbull," Judge Jellico interrupted, "If I grant your petition there's no guarantee that your client will win state titles as a male is there?"

Attorney Pitbull answered, "No there isn't Your Honor, but we'll never find out will we unless he's re-gendered. To be fair this young man is entitled to that opportunity." He felt confident that he hadn't offended the judge with that answer since surely the judge must believe in fairness.

"That's correct Your Honor there is no guarantee," spoke up Jane Doe. "In fact, the guarantee is just the opposite. It's guaranteed that Mr. Pitbull's client will lose his races since his times in both events are over a second slower than all the other male qualifiers at the state finals last year."

"Your Honor, if I may," interrupted Mr. Pitbull, "When my client is changed back into a male, he will be taking male hormone shots. These shots will help him run faster. He'll then be able to compete competitively. He won't be getting female hormone injections anymore."

Attorney Jane Doe rose from her seat. "Your Honor, Cragina has been a female all these years. She thinks like a female. Her hormone shots make her think this way. Her brain has been oriented that way. It cannot be reprogrammed at all, let alone in time for the 'big race.'" She pierced the air mockingly with her first two fingers making the quotation marks and continued. "Her body may become male, but her mind will always be that of a female. If anything, it is cruel and unusual punishment forcing an individual to go through life with two genders, one of the body and one of the mind." Ms. Jane Doe smirked at her adversary as she said this and then sat back down confident that the Judge would not create a two gendered monster. She knew that cruel and unusual punishment didn't apply here because it wasn't a criminal case, but it sounded good, so she used it anyway.

"Miss Doe," said Judge Jellico.

She interrupted him, "It's MS Doe Your Honor."

"Ms. Doe," harrumphed the judge. "What's wrong with being two gendered? Aren't two genders better than one? Two for the price of one so to speak." On occasion the judge enjoyed playing Devil's advocate like now even though he would never rule in favor of what the Devil espoused.

"It would divide the house so to speak Your Honor, divide this child in two. And as you know Your Honor a house divided cannot stand. It must either become all of one or all of the other the other." She said all this confidently since she was quoting from the great Abraham Lincoln, and no one would dare question the wisdom of our illustrious greatest president.

But Judge Jellico didn't think of Abraham Lincoln when he heard that. Instead, when she said 'divide the child', he thought of wise King Solomon of the Bible and the dividing of the baby. He did this as a matter of routine, applying the Bible to the law that is. Maybe if he applied the King Solomon reasoning here one of these two characters would back off like in the Bible and all this nonsense would go away. "Yes." he said to himself after he had momentarily mulled it over in his mind, "Yes that's what Jesus would do and that's what I'm going to do too."

"What say you Mr. Pitbull?" queried the Judge.

Chutney Winston Pitbull was at a loss for words. Secretly he agreed with his opponent, but he couldn't admit that. She had beaten him to the punch, and he was going to have to take that one on the chin so all he could do was to stammer out, "Well that depends, Your Honor." This way he was not committing himself to anything while at the same time leaving the door open to say something later, if he could think of something to say.

Judge Jellico blew some air out of his mouth, flapping his lips as he did so, furrowed his brow and raised his eyes toward the ceiling, then said in a somewhat frustrated and disgusted voice, "Counselors if I could see you two in chambers for a moment, please."

"Yes, Your Honor," came their simultaneous response.

"Counselors," he continued as he sat behind his desk in chambers, the two attorneys in front of him now, "I'm kind of leaning towards this two-gender concept since it will give you both something you want." As a judge he always tried to give each party something in his rulings. This way the attorneys would like him since their clients always got something from him and it made them look good like they had done their jobs and earned their pay. He always threw the loser something even if it was just a bone. But here he didn't think that either attorney would want that type of a solution and since a mother and child's love for each other were at stake certainly one party would back off. If it worked for King Solomon, it should work for him too.

Both attorneys knew how the judge's thought process when deciding cases and both asked if they could have a moment to consult with their clients.

"Take all the time you want counselors," said Judge Jellico, believing that his prayer had been answered, that the wisdom of Solomon would prevail.

MS Doe and her client conferred, and they decided that they would agree that her client's child could be changed to a male but on the further condition that her mind would remain that of a female and that she must continue to receive female hormone injections. That was the most important thing to Olivia. If nothing else she wanted her daughter to think like a woman for the remainder of her minority. It was fall now. There was time enough to get the operation and compete in the spring at the track and field meets. Then her daughter would graduate and turn eighteen that summer. She knew she would have no legal control over her after. She wanted her daughter to be happy and wanted the best for her. So, she would agree to this, a way of salvaging a kind of victory.

Mr. Pitbull and his client conferred too. They were well aware of the timeline also. The youth loved her mother but being a teenager, she was still somewhat selfish. If she could become a male to compete the coming spring, she was willing to leave her mind a female's mind so to speak to accommodate her mother. Besides, she thought that she could figure out a way to counter the female hormones somehow behind her mother's back by getting some male hormones somehow somewhere. As a teenager parental defiance was bound to take precedence. Next fall she or he would be going to college and because of her or his gender or genders he or she thought that some school somewhere would certainly be offering him or her an athletic scholarship of some kind. So, he or she agreed to accept the split gender compromise. And so did Pitbull since he already had been paid in full.

So that is what they agreed to, the body of a male, the mind of a female and they told Judge Jellico this. When he heard it his head and shoulders slumped in disbelief, but he still signed off on the settlement agreement since he had backed himself into a corner by suggesting it and was stuck with it now.

And out in the parking lot afterwards attorney Doe hugged her client and her client's daughter goodbye and Chutney Winston Pitbull lit up a victory cigar, shook his client's hand and wished him well.

And all the while Judge Evan Jellico sat slouched in his chair in his chambers having now convinced himself somehow, that his decision to approve the settlement agreement, was the right thing to do. That the Lord had in fact directed him to approve it. For as he reasoned, the Lord moves in mysterious ways even transgender ways.

So at the next class, like every class to date, the same topics about the story were discussed, symbolism, irony, historical references, humor, tragedy etc. etc. ad nauseam as to these stories.

For the next stories Professor Hillary chose to change the topic from sex to science and gave them four stories concerning science to read, How Mrs. Inuit Saved the Polar Bears, Exodus 21:17, A Pound of Flesh, and The Resurrection of Dr. Muscovy. She had them begin with a story about saving a species.

Chapter Six - How Mrs. Inuit Saved the Polar Bears

Ila Inuit, a widow, lived in the arctic circle with her adult son Yuka. Her husband had accidentally harpooned himself a few years back and was buried and perfectly preserved in the frozen tundra just outside their igloo. There she lived quite contented with her way of life.

But alas all that was about to change and change for the worse. One day her son, while surfing the internet, that's what he did all day, surfed the net just like any normal twenty-seven-year-old who lived at home would do, came upon some very earth-shattering shaking news.

"It says here on the Arctic News Network," he informed his mother, "that due to global warming and or climate change that our friends and neighbors, the polar bears are dying off and facing extinction."

"That's just fake news," his mother responded. "Why just the other day I saw the Polar Bear Family feasting quite contentedly on a cute little baby seal on their own private ice flow."

"But mother it says here that it's dangerous for them to do that. They say big chunks of ice the size of the Sahara Desert are breaking off with polar bears on them and floating so far out to sea that when the polar bears try to swim back to land, they drown. Mother, we must do something to save them before it is too late."

Ila now became concerned. For hadn't she in fact seen the bears on a huge ice floe yesterday. And wasn't it a fact that it was drifting out to sea when she saw them. So, she too started to worry.

"I will go talk to them and see that they are okay and tell them they are endangered or in danger, whatever the case may be," she told her son. "For what the internet says must be true. After all, I have seen it with my very own eyes."

So, Ila went to call on the Polar Bear Family and found that they were okay. So, she informed them that 'some', whoever some are, say that they are endangered species now due to global warming and or climate change and doomed to extinction unless something is done and done soon to save them.

"Just like I suspected," Papa Polar Bear growled. "One of my kin has recently died due to heat stroke. Oh, please save us Mrs. Inuit for we polar bears are a dumb specie. We are not smart like you humans and since your species, not ours, caused this problem, then you as a species are obligated to save us as a specie."

Ila now felt guilty and ashamed of the human race and resolved herself, right then and there, to fix this man-made problem. So, she had Yuka get on the internet to find the answer. He was good with the internet and a good son and was more than glad to help his mother.

Thank God for Al Gore inventing the internet, said Ila to herself as her son began his search. But little did she know that Al Gore had also invented global warming and climate change too.

And all this while global warming and or climate change got only got worser and worser and the polar bears became even more endangered, or in danger, whatever the case may be, for now great white hunters had heard of the soon to be extinction of the polar bears and were flocking in great numbers to the great white north to bag a trophy before they were all gone.

"Mother," Yuka finally announced one morning, after pulling an all-nighter on the net searching for an answer. "I have found a way for you to save the polar bears."

"What is it, my wonderful son?"

"Barbering," he replied. Ila was nonplussed but Yuka then explained his idea to his mother, and she took an online barbering course and got her online barber's license. Then she went off to tell the Polar Bear Family how she would save them all.

"Here's what I am going to do to save you bears," she informed them. "I am a licensed barber now. I will shave each and every one of you so that you are completely hairless just like a Mexican Chihuahua. No hunter will want you for a stuffed trophy or a bear rug since you will look so gross and disgusting, so pinkish with blue blooded veins showing through your transparent skin, visible all over your hairless gross bodies. Why you will look just like a giant mutant hairless pink baby rat. No one wants a rat for a trophy. And in the bargain," she added, "you will be relieved of your heavy fur coats, remain cool, calm and collected, and will not die of heat exhaustion or heat stroke."

"Sounds like a plan," said an enthused Papa Polar Bear. "Let's do it!"

So, Ila went to work and shaved them all and the plan worked for no more hunters sallied forth to kill such gross and disgusting creatures. And the bears and Ila loved it, for after all when a plan comes together, doesn't everyone just love it. So, Ila kept on shaving the bears each month to prevent the growth of their warm thick fur.

But alas the plan came together too good and soon each new generation of baby polar bears born were born with less and less hair. Darwinism had kicked in here, adapting the polar bears bodies to global warming and or climate change.

Now this became upsetting to Papa Polar Bear as he grew old. He was twenty-one years old in bear years, that is ninety-two point four years in human years. He worried that future generations of his kind would never know of the time when polar bears once wore beautiful thick white shiny fur coats and were fierce animals feared by man. So he decided to go to the Ila for the answer to this new problem. For if she solved their problem before, then she could certainly solve this new problem that she had created by fixing the old problem. She owed them that much the way he figured it.

Well as said, global warming was getting worser and worser daily now and it was taking the accelerated course just like all the experts had predicted and the frozen tundra started to thaw and that included the thawing of the body of Ila's husband. Ila became worried again. How was she going to preserve him now that things were changing so rapidly? So, she had Yuka get back on the internet again. And voila he found the answer again. This time it was taxidermy. So, Ila took an online taxidermy course and got her online license to practice taxidermy. Then she stuffed her husband and put him outside her barber shop just like an old fashioned wooden Indian. This way she could be with him each day while she worked yet have him far enough away so that he couldn't bother her like he did when he was alive.

Well on the day she did so, the old Papa Polar Bear came to the shop for a shave and noticed Ila's husband standing outside the door there with a harpoon in his hand, poised ready to throw it. He never cared much for that man. After all her husband had tried to kill him once and he hadn't been all that good with a harpoon anyway. Everyone knew that. But he admired Ila's handy work and the first thing he said to her as he entered her shop was, "I like what you've done with your husband out there. Can you do that to me when I'm gone?"

"Well like the sign on the door says, 'Barber Shop and Taxidermy. I cut 'em or stuff 'em. Your choice'," she giggled.

Papa Polar Bear then sat down in the barber's chair. "Cut me. Don't stuff me. Not just yet anyway," he joked. And then during their idle conversation while she shaved him, Papa Polar Bear told her of his most recent worries about the need to preserve polar bear heritage before they became an entirely different looking species altogether and asked, as nonchalantly as he could, for Ila to help them again.

Now this time Ila did not have to have Yuka go to the internet for an answer. She already knew the answer. Barbering and taxidermy was obviously the combined answer here. So, Ila told Papa Polar Bear that she would save all the fur from him each time she shaved him and then super glue it all back on him when he died. Then she would stuff him and poise him, in a fierce growling snarling position, with sharpened claws extended, in front of her husband outside her shop, so that it looked like Papa Polar Bear was attacking him. Besides, she thought such an oddity would be good for business. But she kept this to herself.

Papa Polar Bear was relieved and overjoyed with that answer and told all his friends and relatives that was what he was going to do with himself when he died. His friends and neighbors liked the idea and pledged themselves to do likewise. Thus polar bear heritage would be preserved so that all future generations of polar bears would know what their ancestors were once a proud, fierce, furred species, not a bunch of pink pantywaist pansies like they were morphing into thanks to Darwinism.

And that's how Mrs. Inuit saved the polar bears, not only from global warming and or climate change and from extinction, but saved, as in the preserved sense of the word, them (as well as her husband), for posterity too.

"Now, as you can see this story is also about climate change. It was a very big issue back then. Today climate change is meaningless of course thanks to the nuclear powered heating and air conditioning drones circling the earth controlling the earth's temperature, cooling it off or heating it up here and there when necessary. But back then there was literally panic in the streets worrying about climate change. The next story assignment also reflects this hysteria, and we will discuss that hysteria next time. Just remember as you read it all the things that I've told you to look for symbolism, comedy, or tragedy, or both, hidden meanings etc. Anyway, you already know what I mean since I passed out that checklist for what to look for. So just check off the item as you discover it. They may be on the test." (Hint. Hint.) "This next story is entitled Exodus 21:17 so note the Biblical references and how the Bible comes into play here and it deals with climate change too."

Chapter Seven - Exodus 21:17

There was an angel named Zacharias who worked for God. His job was to see to it that the minutes changed to hours, the hours to days, days to weeks etc. to etc. And that time marched on uninterrupted as it had for millennials upon millennials here upon the face of God's green earth.

Now some learned people of the planet earth got together and formed a club and called themselves the Lords of Science. And these Lords came to the conclusion, in their infinite wisdom, that man's time, here on earth anyway, was about to run out.

"Man has destroyed the environment of this good earth of ours by his own greed and stupidity and there is nothing that we the learned can do to fix it for you," one of the elite proclaimed. "This planet is long overdue to be hit by asteroids and be destroyed," shouted another. "Global warming will fry the earth and everything upon it," hollered still a third member of the club. And with that said they all chanted in droned unison, "The world will end within one hundred years from today." And they repeated this mantra over and over. But the people did not believe them.

So, the Lords of Science created their own version of time to back up what they had just said. And their version of time wasn't the same as God's. For they had created the Doomsday Clock to prove their point and they set the minute hand thereon a few minutes before midnight. Or was it high noon? It didn't matter anyway for it symbolized that when the clock struck twelve, life here on earth, as we knew it, would end.

The people looked at the clock and became frightened now and shrieked, "What should we do? Where should we go?" And they prostrated themselves before the Lords of Science seeking answers.

So, as to not let a crisis go to waste, and again using their brilliance, the Lords of Science came up with Plan B to live on Planet B. They thought this play on words was clever and that it validated their innate geniusness. Their plan was a simple plan: Move to Planet B. And they told the people of earth of their plan. But secretly the Lords of Science had no intention of taking the people with them when they left.

Now God became angry and upset with such foolishness and conceit by these men. For He deemed it an attempt by them to upstage Him with Science as their god. God meant for mankind's time here on earth to be eternal and never to be ended by man himself. So He sent Zacharias, in a human form, to earth to deliver a message of warning to these so-called learned scientific pharisees.

But these learned ones laughed at Zacharias when they saw him and said unto him, "We do not wish to hear what such a little uneducated man as you has to say for we already know what is best for mankind and have figured it all out." And with that said they shredded the memo from God without even looking at it and sent him away. And this they would live to regret.

Then the Scientists proceeded with their plan to move, and they built a special rocket ship and filled it with all the best and the brightest of the DNA of all the species of flora and fauna, animals and insects, and the different races of man so that they could reproduce them all again on Planet B but only in a better, higher, and much more intelligent life form. And they drew up plans and loaded up materials to build magnificent, aerated bubble pod cities to live in on Planet B because the atmosphere there would not support life as they knew it. And since there was no beauty of nature on Planet B, only a lifeless dull gray dust and rock setting, they would recreate God's beauty of nature in a pod there too but on a much more grander and more beautiful scale than God had done here on earth. And they prided themselves on these their plans of creation.

Then they set the Doomsday Clock at one minute before the stroke of midnight, or high noon, or whatever time it was supposed to be, and then they left earth forever. But before did so, they had already set in motion three earth destroying catastrophes to make sure that the world would end just as they had predicted. For if it did not, then they would look foolish, and their work would have all been in vain and vain people cannot can not accept results such as foolishness and failure.

Now God knew what the Lords of Science had planned. For God knows all that goes on in the minds of his children and He sent Zacharias to earth again. This time with the knowledge and instructions on how to thwart the plans of these evil men. For God too had a plan.

First the Lords of Science had employed teams of men all over the world to use giant jack hammers on all the fault lines of earth so that the earth would open up and split apart and all of mankind would be swallowed up therein and die as a result thereof. So, Zacharias went to the places of the giant jackhammers and told the men there that he was from the Lords of Science and that their instructions were wrong and instead of jack hammering the earth apart they were to drill into the earth for oil. This made more sense to these men. So, they began to drill for oil and God made oil bubble forth from their drilling, enriching not only them, but all of mankind with lower gas prices.

Second, the Lords of Science had built and sent into space a giant asteroid and programmed it to collide with the earth destroying the entire planet. So, Zacharias went to the military generals of the earth and told them this and the generals sent forth powerful missiles and destroyed the asteroid thousands of miles above the earth's surface blowing it into a fine powdery dust. And God blessed that dust and had it settle on the ozone layer above the earth destroying the ozone layer and thus saving the earth from the deadly greenhouse effect.

Third, the Lords of Science had built an artificial drone sun with nuclear heating powers and had sent it high above the earth to heat the earth to the point where the oceans would boil and all life forms on land would be charred and fried beyond recognition. So, Zacharias went to the Temple of Science, found the controls for the drone, and shut it off. Then God had Zacharias reprogram it so that the atmosphere could be mildly heated or cooled whenever and wherever it best suited man. And He had Zacharias program the artificial sun to produce wind and rain patterns over certain areas on earth that were presently unproductive so as to make those areas fruitful and bear crops. And all of mankind benefited greatly from the reprogrammed artificial sun.

All this was unbeknownst of course to the Lords of Science who were thousands of light years from earth at the time as they made their exodus through the vastness of space.

Now while doing so, they came upon an asteroid storm and God saw it and parted the asteroids for their ship to pass through. But when the ship reached the eye of the storm, God closed the asteroid storm around them, and rained down His wrath upon these men, destroying them and all their learning.

And God thus having accomplished His plan, He drew Zacharias back up to Heaven with Him. And Zacharias went back to work making sure that time marched on, just as it always had, for millennia upon millennia, world without end. Amen.

The class was fascinated by this Biblical type of story. A lot of the students had no idea what the Bible was and had never heard of it. Some of them even went to the trouble and looked it up and came to the conclusion that it was another book of fairy tales to be discovered and studied and suggested to Professor Hillary that she chose some stories from it for the class to read. But she reminded them that this class was about 21st century fairy tales not Biblical prehistoric fairy tales. And so as to get away from the enthrallment with the Bible she chose as her next story, 'The Tax Against Sodas'. It dealt with governmental regulations based on scientific research which she emphasized were a big deal back then not like today where they are just a way of life.

Chapter Eight - The Tax on Sodas

The Tax on Sodas

Nanny Goatosi was the mayor pro bono uber alles of Animalville. The city was in desperate need of money, as always, and the only way it could get more was to tax something. So, the mayor had decided to tax sodas because everyone drinks sodas and therefore lots of moola would come rolling into the city feed troughs. Thus, the proposal now before the city council was to tax soda. It was only a question of how much, for it had been scientifically proven, through government funded scientific research studies, that soda was ruining children's teeth, but worse than that it was making them fat. So, fat in fact that children were dying in the streets from obesity. Fatness or obesity, now politically correctly being called 'overweight impaired,' had reached epidemic proportions here just like the Black Plague had once done so and ravaged Europe eons ago. Thus, it was inevitable that the tax was going to be enacted for who in their right mind does not want to save the poor helpless children. After all there were constant ads on tv to save the starving emaciated children all over the world and therefore it only made sense, seemed logical and fitting that fat children should be saved too.

But not everyone agreed. Council Animal Oyster Shyster was one who didn't. Didn't believe anyway that they should be saved that way. He was a lawyer and therefore trained to look at all sides of an issue, and even to advocate in these trying challenging unparalleled unprecedented times, all sides of an issue, but especially the side that favored him the most. After all this was a crisis and it should not go to waste.

Also, Council Animal Peggy Porker looked at only one side, her side and those of her porky puercos constituents of the Pig Parlor Ward. She was against the tax for her constituents lived to consume, consume all kinds of food items and beverages. They weren't willing to pay any price or bear any burden, for after all they were pigs, not bears, that denied them their constitutional right to their pursuit of porcine happiness.

However, the rest of the Animal Council were all Democats and being so knew what was best for everyone, whether everyone liked what was best for themselves or not. Here they were doing the right thing, protecting the children. For after all didn't a famous Democat once said, "Ask not what you can do to your government but what your government can do to you."

"Okay let's vote on it now," baah-ed Nanny Goatosi knowing that she had enough votes now to ram it through.

"Hold on there a minute, Mayor. Aren't you getting the cart before the horse here," spoke up Shyster. "Why we haven't even read or discussed the proposed tax and that is a required legal requirement that must be legally fulfilled before we can make anything legal, otherwise it automatically becomes illegal."

"Mr. Shyster," whined the mayor, "we can read it and discuss it later but first we have to pass it in order to read and discuss it."

"No law can be nunc pro tunc Ms. Mayor," said Shyster, impressing everyone with his legalese.

"Yah that's right," grunted Peggy Porker, popping open a can of Mountain Dew in direct violation and defiance of the no food and drinks at the table while the council is in session rule.

"Nunc pro tunc can be done later too," groaned the Mayor. She didn't know nunc pro tunc from ex post facto but she bleated that out anyway. "We must do this for the children. We can't let them get fat." Then she threw in for good measure, "It takes a village you know."

"For the children? Really Ms. Mayor isn't this about raising money," snarked Oyster as he smiled his smirky smile. His teeth were perfect and were shiny pearly white. They sparkled and glistened. He brushed with Gleam or con Gleem as they say in Spanish.

Peggy Porker finished swallowing her Twinkie, washed it down with a slug of Mountain Dew and then burped out, "But what about my constituents. They are genetically programmed to be fat. Drinking less soda ain't gonna change them none, Dearie. All it'll do is cost them more money. They ain't gonna swallow all this hogwash you're trying to ram down their throats."

"Well it won't hurt them anyway then will it if they're born to be fat," reasoned the mayor. "Maybe we should tax that Twinkie too there you just wolfed down since you 'weight overloaded impaired' animals are going to buy them anyway." Mayor Goatosi was frustrated with all this debate nonsense business and at her wits end, which wasn't all that long to start with, and could think of nothing else to say, so she said the obvious. "Let's vote now!"

"Hold your horses there again Madam Mayor. I have a better proposal," said Shyster, for his brightest and best legal mind had just come up with another way to raise funds for the city and at the same time for himself too of course. "Let's make it against the law to sell soda to minors. After all, kids can't buy beer and one can of soda is much more harmful to a child than a can of beer is, or even a six pack for that matter. Make it illegal to sell to minors and fine the hell out of someone or company, like McCownald's for instance, that does. Then hire an attorney to collect the fine."

Mayor Goatosi stopped to think about it. It took a while but soon it was plain for all to see that the light bulb above her head came on. Though it was rather dimly lit.

"That's right McCownald's, Harvee's (named so for the Pooka), Burger-LIke-Food, they're all the bad guys here," she said. "Ruining our children by serving sugar sodas, getting them all buzzed up, destroying the enamel of their teeth costing parents thousands in dental bills besides and making them fat with cowlarie laden burgers and fries. Yeah, these are the guys we gotta get."

"We need to fine them if they sell soda to minors. Fine 'em big time," shouted a fired-up lawyer Shyster.

"Why can't we just tell our kids no." spoke up Peggy. "Like when my kids start pigging out and hogging all the food. I just pull them away from the food trough and tell them no more. Just say 'No'. It's that simple."

"That might work for drugs," rebuked the mayor, "but it won't work here because kids are more addicted to sugar than drugs. Sugar is a more powerful. We need to make it against the law to sell, serve, or even give a soda to a minor. That way if McCownald's does, we can fine them a million dollars per occurrence. After all they can afford it."

"On second thought," said Shyster, hoping to implement the money-making scheme he had already concocted in his feverish lawyer mind, "maybe this isn't a good idea after all. We might be creating a black market for soda. We would need a special office, a special agency then like the FBI, CIA, MIC, KEY,MO, or USE to combat that too, to bust and fine bootleggers"

"You're right again Mr. Shyster," piped up the mayor, "well we'll just have to create that special agency, with special neat cool letters and pay for it out of the million dollar fines we collect so it doesn't cost us any additional money. These fast-food companies can afford a couple of million dollar fines here and there. After all their dumb teenage employees are bound to screw up and serve their homie friends soda. It won't hurt McCownald's none and this way we get lots of money from a golden goose, well actually lots of golden gooses. Oyster, you're a legal eagle genius. Why you'd be just the person to head up the agency and collect the fines."

"Well," said Shyster thinking on his feet, for that is what good lawyers do, think on their feet that is, but he already knew what he was going to say here. "How about a fifty percent contingency fee?"

"Better make the fine two million then," joked Peggy, "so that the attorneys can suck on the public you know what then and the city still gets its original million."

"I second that motion," Oyster Shyster blurted out.

"So be it then, the motion is passed," said Mayor Goatosi. "Draw it all up Mr. Shyster and I'll sign it tomorrow."

"Ms. Mayor," said Peggy.

"Yes Peggy."

"The candy machine in the hall took my money and I didn't get anything. Can I get my money back?"

"Bring it up at the next meeting dear. This meeting is adjourned."

"Well," said Professor Hillary. "The government does know what's best for you as to what to hear but it also knows what's best for you to say or not say as our next story so indicates.

Chapter Nine - A Pound of Flesh

The whole village was up in arms that night. They were demanding their pound of flesh. A town hall meeting had been hurriedly called by the village board the purpose of which was to distance themselves as far as possible from the mayor and to let their fellow citizens know that they did not approve of, nor stand for the things that he had recently said. The town hall had soon filled to overflow capacity and spilled out into the streets becoming an angry and unruly mob, for after all, what good is a mob if it's not angry and unruly. It was a stark and swarmy mob that night that ranted and raved under a full moon brandishing their pitchforks, scythes, clubs and torches, howling for justice, for their pound of flesh.

Hizzoner the mayor, Wally Walrus, was under siege. He had committed the unpardonable capital offense of making derogatory remarks about a couple of gays. Gay warthogs that is after he lost a local contest to them. The local paper, The Animal Animus, had run a Valentine's Day cutest couple picture contest and awarded the prize of a hundred dollar gift certificate from the local feed store to a gay warthog couple. The paper did so to show solidarity with and support for the gay community for that was the cool and hep cat thing to do.

Wally had entered his picture with himself and his life partner, that is his shack up honey, Walinda, a woman of huge proportions like himself but without a mustache. She had shaved it off for the contest. Not very feminine like for a female to have a big droopy mustache. Didn't look cute.

Now nobody here is saying that warthogs are cuter than walruses or vice versa. For cuteness like beauty is in the eye of the beholder, and with warthogs and walruses much cuteness is left to be desired. But in this case, in the eye of the newspaper, the beholder here, the warthogs won.

Good ole boy Wally took offense at losing and said some disparaging words while in his sore loser mode. The village was not used to such words. For seldom was heard a disparaging word there. But their skies were cloudy some days.

The gist and jelly of his statement was as follows. "These freaking gays all look alike. You can't tell the males from the females. The men want to look like women and the women like men. They all really need to be transgenderized. Maybe even tenderized." Wally had fouled his own village nest with these words. Very disparaging words indeed.

The drive by media had picked up on all this and ran with it. They were there in full force tonight along with all the gay, lesbian, and transsexual organizations from all over the world, vultures ready to feast on every disparaging word. (Have we said disparaging enough?)

The village board consisted of Timothy Titmouse, Bonita Burro, and Iggie Inuit. They sat on stage along with the mayor and his attorney Oyster Shyster. The resolution that the board had already decided on and passed, all this being done at the Monkey Shines Inn last night and in violation of the Open Meetings Act, was: "We hereby remove the mayor from office for saying such offensive and definitely not p.c. things."

Timothy Titmouse was the shy, timid, tepid type but he had political ambitions, so he volunteered to conduct the meeting that night. But true to form he hesitated too long and Attorney Oyster Shyster, true to form, jumped up, grabbed the microphone and began talking, or rather telling.

"May I remind the board that the board has no authority under the laws of this state to remove a sitting mayor from office. There is no statute that allows you to do that," he bellowed his hands grasping his lapels as he rocked back on his heels and smiled his smirky smile. His teeth were pearly white like his suit for he wanted to come across as a good guy and good guys always wore white.

Now Iggie Inuit jumped up from his seat in response. Iggie was a climate change global warming refugee from the Arctic wasteland who had settled here after climate change and global warming had killed off all the cold weather animals, caribou, seals, and dare we say walruses, that he counted on for his food supply. "Well if that is the law, then the law is an," and then stopped cold in his tracks before he finished that famous Shakespearean quote. Bonita Burro had just shot him a dirty look. He had almost offended the burro, donkey, mule, pack animal or whatever they called themselves community. Not a p.c. thing to do. He wisely backed off, shut up and sat down.

"Remember that my client has a right to free speech, a right to his own opinion no matter how unpopular or offensive that opinion may be," boldly continued Shyster.

"Well, your big blubbery client has no right to disgrace our village," shot back Iggie. For some reason or another there was bad blood between Iggie and Wally. They didn't much care for each other.

Oyster Shyster smiled his pearly white smile at the crowd again. His teeth were perfect. He said one word, "Lawsuit."

The crowd hushed up with a deafening silence.

"Treble Damages," he continued. Oh, Shyster would make certain that he sued for treble damages alright. He'd put it in his fee contract with Walrus that he, Shyster that is, got to keep the treble damages as his fee. That's where the money was to be made here.

"Treble damages mean damages awarded in addition to actual damages in the amount of three times actual damages. Commonly referred to as ``punitive damages." Shyster had them on the ropes now.

The crowd reeled back on its collective heels in fear. They didn't want to pay no treble damages.

"This could bankrupt the village," someone hollered.

"Raise our taxes to pay for a lawsuit we don't need," screamed another.

"Tie us up in court for years," said yet another.

Timothy Titmouse had been sitting there this whole time working up his courage to speak. He wanted to be mayor and he couldn't let Shyster bully his village anymore. This was his opportunity. He couldn't let this crisis go to waste. He knew the answer here and knew that it would help him get elected mayor next election. So timidly he spoke up. "Best to let him stay and vote him out in the next election," he squeaked. "That's the answer here. And oh by the way I'm running for mayor," he announced.

The crowd went into murmur mode and the consensus was that Titmouse had come up with the perfect solution. Walrus was up for reelection this coming fall. Vote him out. That was the cheapest simplest thing to do. Everyone was nodding their heads in agreement.

Oyster Shyster saw his potential fee slipping away. He had to act fast. So, thinking on his feet, which is what all good lawyers are trained to do, especially when it comes to their fee, he said something in haste that he shouldn't have said. Something that would come back to bite him in the butt big time.

"Oh, that's okay," he said smugly. "We'll just challenge the election and get the results thrown out. Will file suit in California. We'll still get treble damages."

The crowd had had enough. It appeared that no matter what they did, Shyster was going to sue. Enough is enough already. It was time for action. No shyster lawyer named Shyster was going to push them around.

"The hell with all this lawyer talk anyway," screamed someone. "We need justice now! Tonight!"

"Let's do it," someone else shouted. And with that the crowd rose as one and lurched forward toward the stage and Walrus. Revenge was about to be served, hot or cold, it didn't matter.

Walrus sensed the ugly mood of the resurrected mob and ran, lumbered that is, toward the door. He was a big fellow and got stuck in the doorway. In fact, when he first entered he had to turn sideways to slip through with the help of some whale oil rubbed on his big bulging blubbery belly.

The mob was a tsunami of a wave and couldn't stop. They crashed into Walrus shoving him through the door and collectively fell on top of him. Wally fell facedown causing his two sharp pointed tusks to puncture his chest. The mobsters climbed off of him and rolled him over. He was still alive.

"Kill him!" someone shouted. "Kill him!" he hollered again, waving his arm and imitating William Holstein from the movie The Bridge on the River Cowai.

Iggie Inuit stepped forward, harpoon in hand, he had brought it for the riot, and after a number of well-placed thrusts Wally Walrus was dead. Actually, more thrusts were made than necessary but only an Inuit would know that.

"What do we do with him now?" someone asked.

"Chop him into pieces like in Apocalypse Cow," the movie aficionado screamed.

Thus, Oyster Shyster saw his fee, a pile of still warm jiggling blubber, hauled away by the village tow truck to the Monkey Shines Inn where Wally was barbecued and served up to the public at a fundraiser for future village legal fees.

It was Iggie's idea to do all this. He loved walrus meat. A good time was had by all. The village had gotten its pounds of flesh.

And as to Attorney Shyster and his fee, well the board gave him a pound of flesh, barbequed blubber meat that is.

And when Shyster bit into his former client at the fundraiser he remarked, "Tastes like chicken."

"Nah tastes like seal," corrected Iggie.

"What's seal taste like?" Shyster asked.

"Chicken," Iggie mumbled, munching a mouthful.

"Well class," began Professor Hillary again as she always did at her next class, "you can see from that tale that certain things were said back then that today we would not even dream of saying."

That was true. For no longer was anyone ever offended by offensive speech since everyone now thought and spoke alike on all issues. This of course makes for the better homogenous society that we have today.

The class mumbled their approval to their teacher's remark for none of them had ever been offended in their entire life. And because of this it was hard for them to identify with the characters and feel their pain.

The last story, The Resurrection of Dr. Muscovy, proved that even science run amok, became a reality.

Chapter Ten - The Resurrection of Dr. Muscovy

The good doctor, Dr. Ivanstein Muscovy, was dead. Well, he wasn't really a good doctor, more of an inept weird kind of doctor, and definitely not a purposely evil doctor that's for sure, but regardless of what kind of doctor he was, he was still dead, and now they had to do something with his body. They being his two assistants, Igor, as he was called, the horribly deformed, ugly, but faithful assistant and Ilsa, the young beautiful blonde lovely assistant.

Igor was called that, Igor that is, because Dr. Muscovy had placed an ad in the Kansan Crier, the local flyer, that read: "Wanted faithful obedient assistant for scientific experiments. No experience necessary. Will train using Pavlovian method. Must be horribly deformed, if not, must consent to become so, and must answer to the name of Igor." So 'Igor' applied. His real name was Pat, but he needed the work to feed his family of six still back in Cuernavaca, Mexico which he hoped to bring to this country soon before the wall went up. He was somewhat deformed, but not that much, so he agreed to let Dr.Muscovy operate on him to make him completely so in order to get the job.

Ilsa, was called Ilsa because she had answered Dr. Muscovy's other ad which read. "Wanted beautiful young blonde with bright blue eyes and long flowing flaxen hair for job as a lovely laboratory assistant. Must be of Scandinavian descent and must agree to be called Ilsa." The doctor liked the name Ilsa since it reminded him of his days in Paris and Casablanca. "Duties include handing sharp scissors and other sharp instruments for the doctor and posing provocatively while doing so. Uniform of short white mini skirt and a low-cut front white blouse will be provided."

Gina, that was Ilsa's real name, was a gypsy and was tired of being pawed at all the time at her job as a waitress at the Dish and Spoon Diner. She had been looking to run away from there for some time now and this was her chance. So, she got out her Dolly Parton wig and ironed it out until it was completely flat and no longer had any big flowing curls left in it, bought some blue eye contacts, took a Swedish accent course on the internet, tarted herself up, and got the job.

"What should we do with him?" whined Ilsa. "Who do we notify, Igor? He has no relatives in this country."

"Well, we certainly don't notify the authorities. That's for sure," said Igor. "The man was in this country illegally, you know."

That was true. Dr. Muscovy had fled the ravages of Europe after World War II and entered this country as an unapproved illegal alien. He'd changed his appearance physically, as he had given himself a complete body makeover from head to toe and changed his name too. No one knew who he really was, or where he came from, and that was the way the doctor liked it, and so did Igor and Ilsa for that matter too.

"Well, it's a shame he's gone," said Ilsa. "He was such a wonderful man having done all those wonderful scientific experiments for the wonderment of mankind. All his work down the toilet now, flushed forever into the sewers of life." She loved waxing poetically.

Igor had half a brain left, or at least he thought so, after Dr.Muscovy removed part of it for a brain transplant to that blankety blank monster he had created and something now began to stir in what was left of it.

"Remember that monster he created, Franken something or other, like Al Frankenstein or something like that. Remember that part about the brain transplant Ilsa?"

Ilsa was nonplussed.

"You know. You handed the doctor sharp instruments then. Remember?"

"Oh yeah," she answered as the light bulb above her head came on. "Say whatever happened to that guy anyway?"

"The local farmers here chased him to the top of the Bunge grain elevator, he fell in and was augured out into a railway car mixed in with the wheat. No one ever heard grain or chaff from him again."

"It's a shame we can't bring the doctor back to life like the way he brought that Al Franken guy back," sighed Ilsa.

And then the light bulb connected the dots in Igor's head.

"Oh, but we can my whirling gypsy dancer. All that life giving stuff is stored in the doctor's brain. You know stuff like how to strap a guy down, wire him up, and expose him to lightning so that he gets jolted back to life. Stuff like that."

"So, all we have to do is pick his brain?" asked Ilsa, her face contorting as she did so.

"Not exactly my tell all tarot card reader. We do a brain transplant. We transfer his brain to you so that you can then regurgitate all that stuff about how to make the dead come back to life to me so that I can reactivate the doctor."

"But what do we do with my brain?" asked Ilsa. "Throw it away? I might want it back someday, you know."

"Why we simply put it in the doctor so that he will have a brain in him when we bring him back to life again. And then when he's alive, and here he emoted and repeated the words 'He's alive!', I do another transplant. He gets his brain back and you get yours."

"Huh?" huhed Ilsa.

"Exactamundo my jingling jiggling tambourine twirler. Now where the heck are those notes of his on brain transplanting anyway? Help me find them please."

Well, they found the doctor's notes. They were illegible handwritten notes of course and who can ever read a doctor's signature, let alone many pages of handwritten medical procedural instructions. But Igor was not discouraged in the least as he remembered some of the procedure from the time when the doctor transplanted his brain. Thus, undaunted he plunged ahead, meaning he plunged a needle into the head of Ilsa injecting her baby brain with novocaine so that he could remove it from her without her feeling any pain. For after all that was the humane thing to do. He then set up recording cameras to tape the operation for training film purposes, and for quality assurance, and to copyright and sell it at a later date. Then he proceeded with the operation.

The operation was a success. Ilsa got the doctor's brain and the doctor got Ilsa's brain, for now anyway. Igor was kind of in a hurry now, so when done he cauterized both incisions with a blowtorch and rather than take the time to stitch their skulls back up, he superglued the hacksawed pieces of their skulls back in place and hopefully got the right pieces to the right head, and then taped it all up with duct tape. Duct tape being the deranged scientist's secret weapon.

Then a few minutes later, when Ilsa had fully recovered, he had her recall the procedure to bring the dead back to life. But when she explained to him how many watts of electricity were needed to be transfused through the human body to do so, Igor knew there was a problem. He did a quick mental calculation in his head, after all where else does one mentally calculate but in one's head and realized that even if he stuck all of the doctor's fingers and toes, and even his nose and other body parts in the electrical sockets here in the lab there still wouldn't be enough volts to bring him back to life. The doctor would just not get that one big jolt of electricity that he would need to make him come alive. Like the jolt one gets from one's first cup of coffee and cigarette in the morning or from LSD.

So disappointingly and mournfully he told Ilsa that there was nothing they could do to bring their doctor back to the land of the living.

But Ilsa was not ready to give up yet. So, she asked, "Why can't we just have him get struck by lightning during the next storm?"

Igor explained. The problem was that they were in Kansas. They wished they weren't in Kansas anymore, but they were. They wished they were high in the Carpathian Mountains somewhere in Transylvania in a medieval castle with a lift to expose the body high to the heavens and have it struck by lightning on a dark and stormy night. For that was the kind of place to truly conduct an experiment such as this. Not here on the flat plains of Kansas where the highest building in the little burg of Limitless Prairie Kansas, population 409, was the Bunge Grain Elevator.

And that couldn't be used for three reasons. First there was no privacy there. The kids were always bungee jumping from it, and not all that successfully too, as they always ended up slamming into the sides of the concrete grainery knocking their teeth out. They did wear helmets though. And second, even if they got the body up there it wouldn't make any difference anyway because it didn't rain in Kansas anymore thanks to global change climate warming.

And third, even if it did rain, all that excitement would be just too much for these Kansas Jayhawkers and they would amass as a crowd of rubbernecking, gawking, slack jawed, tobacco spitting hayseed farmers, spitting, and dribbling chewing tobacco juice all down the front of their bib overalls and wiping their toothless gummy mouths and chins with red bandana handkerchiefs while waiting for the show to begin. And that was a sight Igor and Ilsa did not wish to even envision let alone witness in person.

"So, what do we do?" whined Ilsa.

"Well, we start looking for a job," said a deflated Igor. He had so hoped to inflate the doctor back to life. "Yes, that's what we do, since it doesn't appear now that we can bring Doctor back to life." He sighed and emoted painfully as he dropped his chin to his chest. Then there on the floor he espied, yes that's right espied, the Kansan Crier. He picked it up and turned to the Help Wanted section.

His bug eyes lit up and bugged out at the same time, he was good at multitasking, as he read the following ad: "Wanted Executioner and Assistant for annual Electro Fest. Duties include strapping down the doomed, throwing the switch, and removing and disposing of the dead bodies. Assistant need not be lovely. Apply at the Obama Health Care Center in Capital City." Electrocutions were now covered under the new and improved free health care act and the Obama Care people were in charge of them under the death panel provisions therein.

"Here's the answer," Igor announced. "Read this," he said pointing to the ad. "This is how we resurrect the body of Dr.Muscovy. There's got to be enough juice in one of them there electric chairs to bring him back to life. If it can kill, it only makes sense it can bring one back to life too. It's our last and only chance. We've got to do it for the doctor."

Ilsa read it.

"I don't know," she whined. "I might be too lovely for that job. Overqualified you know."

Well Igor convinced her she wasn't that lovely after all and this kind of hurt her feelings some, but she got over it and agreed to go with him to Capital City and apply for the job.

Electro Fest was an annual festival of electric executions combined with the traditions of an old-world beer drinking, sausage and sauerkraut swallowing, German Oktoberfest. Kansas had been settled by a lot of Germans, like the Eisenhower family for example, and this was a way for the locals to get touchy feely with their heritage roots. Well anyway it was soon approaching, so all three of them set out that night down the yellow concreted road for the emerald Capital City. Igor explained his plan along the way.

Igor's plan was simple. The state's electric chair would provide enough jolts of electricity to bring Dr.Muscovy back to life, just like him getting hit with bolts of lightning. He was sure of that now since he looked it up on the internet. So somehow, while executing people, they would strap the doctor into the electric chair, and jolt him back to life again.

Well needless to say they got the jobs. Ilsa went as Gina so she wouldn't be too lovely, and Igor used his real name too, of Pat O'Brien, spelled Patricio Obregon in Mexican.

Electro Fest drew thousands just as public hangings used to back in the days of the wild wild west at Dodge City. Ten days of family fun. Family ticket packs sold out quickly and besides the money the state charged for admission, the state put the electrocutions on pay per view television at an outrageous price but a price the public gladly paid, nonetheless. The whole thing was a moneymaker for the state and a source of fundraising for local churches, boy and girl scout troops, little league, other charitable organizations and of course 4-H. They all lined the streets with their kiosks selling pastries, fast food, soft drinks, and raffle tickets.

Well, the first nine days went by quickly and all the electrocutions of any interest had expired. The maniacal, mass, psycho, and serial killers had all been killed off and all that was left for Sunday's executions, Sunday being the last day, were a couple of run of the mill 'I got drunk' or 'I was high on drugs' or 'I must have blacked out' murderers. So, the pay for view network, ESPN, Electrocutions, Sports and Politics Network, did not broadcast them that Sunday morning. Besides everybody in Kansas went to church on Sunday morning and wouldn't be watching tv anyway, unless watching a tv evangelist of course. So, Sunday was the day that Pat O'Brien and Gina would save Dr. Muscovy.

Pat, aka, Igor, and Ilsa, aka Gina, were poised and ready to act when they brought in the last doomed one, a huge dumb former football player who killed another football player while committing the football offense of unnecessary roughness. He was penalized fifteen yards for that in addition to receiving the death penalty. Igor and Ilsa went to work and double dosed this guy, just to make sure, and when the State Coroner pronounced him DOA, they hurried all the governmental authorities, box office seat witnesses, and the deceased's mother out the front door. Then from the back door they hauled in Dr. Muscovy, strapped him to the chair, and double dosed him too, again to make sure, and waited. And sure, enough after a couple of minutes of haunting moaning and groaning, Dr. Ivanstein Muscovy came back to life.

"It's alive!" they shouted miraculously simultaneously as Dr. Muscovy started to groggily wake up, unstrap himself and rise from the dead. And just as he did so the football player's momma re-entered the room to hurl some more curses and insults at her dead son and upon seeing the doctor coming alive, she let out an eerie ear-piercing screech, put the back of her right hand against her forehead, whirled around in dramatic fashion, keeled over backwards, and fainted.

Ilsa took charge now. Remember she still had the Dr. Muscovy brain in that skull of hers. "Hurry now," she commanded Igor. "I'll assist the doctor out to the hearst mobile, and you bring the dead body and load it in the back with the others. Let's get out of here before anything else happens." Ilsa knew the doctor would want all those bodies for future experiments. So that is why she saved them.

They drove far into the dark and stormy night towards home and as they did so Ilsa explained to Dr. Muscovy all that had happened since he accidentally gave himself a heart attack and died during one of his self-injecting experiments. Another failed experiment gone awry obviously.

The population of Limitless Prairie Kansas rose to 431 that next morning as Igor unloaded the carcasses of the electrocuted. Then Ilsa took charge again.

"Now doctor," said Ilsa. "Igor must do a reverse brain transplant and transfer your brain back to you and my brain back to me."

Dr. Muscovy was about to say something when Ilsa cut him off and barked out, "Okay everybody let's get started now." And then in her best Chinese, "Chop. Chop," and clapped her hands twice.

Igor started to scrub up, but Dr. Muscovy went over to him, put his hand on Igor's shoulder, and told him to stop. Then told them both that he kind of liked having a female brain as he had been trying to get in touch with his feminine side for some time now. Told them that he had also been thinking about doing sex change operations. That they were the next big money makers and having a female of the specie brain in him would give him first-hand knowledge of what it's all about to be a woman and roar and would be quite helpful to him in the sex change business.

"But doctor," warned Ilsa. "If you go around here acting girly, people will think you're weird."

But Dr. Muscovy insisted on keeping Ilsa's brain. So, after Igor and Ilsa consulted with each other, they decided that it was his life and they should not try to alter it, except if he was dead of course. Then Igor offered the doctor some advice.

"Well maybe you should move to the Granola state," he proposed.

"Huh?" huuhed Dr. Muscovy channeling Ilsa's brain.

"You know Californy. The land of fruit and nuts. You'd fit right in out there with all those other pre-transexual druggy weirdos."

Well Dr. Muscovy realized that Californy was the place he ought to be, so he loaded up his truck and he moved hurriedly. To fruit cake land that is, movie stars, left wing loonies, (same thing).

Ilsa and Igor remained in the fields of creams, Cream of Wheat and Farina, that is, Kansas, the land of hot bland breakfast cereals.

Ilsa was the brains of the outfit now and Igor remained as her faithful servant, for after all that was what he was trained to do, and he wasn't qualified to do anything else but electrocute people and that was only a part time job each year at Electro Fest.

But Ilsa now wanted a new assistant as Igor wasn't all that pleasant to look at. So, she placed a help wanted ad on the internet which read: "Wanted Hunky Young Male Assistant to assist lovely female doctor in life conducting scientific experiments. Duties include being hunky, photogenic and posing provocatively. Must agree to be

80

called 'Incredible Hunk.' No experience necessary. Will train."

Igor could see the writing on the wall, or as here, see the writing on the internet since he had hacked into Dr. Ilsa's computer. She called herself doctor now. So, Igor lit out for Californy to join Dr. Muscovy and was looking forward to assisting him in the sex change business and collecting certain body parts.

And Ilsa, well she got her hunky assistant after all. His real name was Millard. But he liked being called Incredible Hunk. He wasn't all that smart either but that was okay with her as she liked that in a man, not being too smart that is.

And so thus ends the story of how Igor and Ilsa, the ugly and the lovely, resurrected Dr. Muscovy. A storybook ending in which they all lived ever so happily, ever so after, each in their ever so own personal and perverted ways.

"What this story points out," said Professor Hillary, "is that what we once thought impossible has become the possible. Dr. Muscovy and his forerunner Dr. Frankenstein were fictitious characters back then but are real today. In this sense, literature can become the forerunner, the foreseer of the future.

Now for next time we are going to switch gears and deal with a president of the early twenty first century and how he came to make us what we are today. They'll be a pro story and then a con story about him and then a story comparing him to his predecessors. The pro story is first and of course it never happened so please read Paying For The Wall First, then The Business of Being King, which never happened either unfortunately, and then Rocky and Bullwinkle Discuss Their Presidents.

Chapter Eleven - Paying for The Wall

Don K. Haughty was the ruler of his kingdom. He had got elected as such by promising to build a wall between his kingdom and the kingdom to the south, the kingdom of Senior Max Amigo. He further vowed that he would make Max Amigo pay for it, the cost of the wall that is. Needless to say, the two were not friends.

So fearful that he would make an ass of himself if he didn't keep his campaign promise, Don K. began constructing the wall.

Max Amigo defiantly laughed at Don K.Haughty. "You are on a fool's errand," he taunted. "The windmills of your mind must not be turning for we will never pay." Max Amigo wanted no wall to be built for he viewed an open border as a safety valve, that is a solution for all the problems of his kingdom that he could not fix.

Don K. Haughty paid no attention to this bravado for such boasting was typical of Max Amigo. Just more southerly hot air he thought. So, he charged onward and as said, he began construction. Or so he said he did. But there was nothing there to see, no great impressive wall like the Great Wall of China, no drab concrete barbed wire topped wall like the Berlin Wall, nothing but a few antenna towers spaced intermittently along the entire border. That is certainly not a wall thought Max Amigo.

Then one day Don K.Haughty announced, "The wall is done and now Max Amigo it is time that you paid for your haughtiness."

Max Amigo looked across the border. His view was unobstructed. "Pay for what," he laughed. "There is nothing there. I see no wall."

"Oh but it is a magic wall," bragged Don K.Haughty. "You can not see it, but it is there all the same. Trust me."

"Trust you. Ha!" I will prove that no such 'magical wall' exists. Max Amigo then ordered his faithful servant, Poncho Sanza, to cross over the border and walk through this invisible wall into the Kingdom of Don K. Haughty.

Poncho Sanza was a trusting but scared soul as he approached the wall. He believed in magic and hesitated one step short of the border wall.

"Do it!" ordered Max Amigo for he did not tolerate disobedience from his peons.

More scared of Max Amigo than of magic Poncho Sanza stepped forward and instantly was zapped to Jesus, like a bug zapped by a bug zapper, nothing remained of him anywhere. He was gone.

"See the wall is magic like I said," boasted Don K.Haughty. "It will zap all you pesky blood sucking mosquitoes that try to cross it."

Max Amigo hesitated. He thought it politically best not to order another of his servants into the 'wall' that wasn't there.

Don K. Haughty chuckled to himself. The wall he had built was a Star Wars wall. The technology thereof had been developed and used against a former enemy of his kingdom, by a former ruler of the kingdom, many years ago. So, Don K. Haughty decided to employ it here too. It had cost him nothing since it already existed. Nevertheless, he hollered back to Max Amigo, "Now you will pay."

Maximus Leon Amigo defiantly roared back, "We will never pay."

But alas poor Max Amigo paid dearly. For now, the peons of his kingdom were unable to leave a life of grinding poverty, drug cartels, and overcrowding. They could not flee to the north to a better life since the wall would certainly kill them. So, they were doomed. Yet they continued to breed like bunnies, exacerbating the problem as they were not genetically programmed like lemmings to kill themselves when their numbers got too large. And as for the criminals of the country, they could no longer escape justice by fleeing north. So, they stayed and wreaked further havoc on the denizens of the kingdom. Nor could the drug dealers move their merchandise now, for it was certain death to try to cross the border. So, they were forced to sell their drugs at lower prices, to the peons. This was because the peons, though they craved the drugs for the illusionary temporary escape that it provided them, had very little dinero to spend on drugs. Thus, the price dropped and the drug dealers became poorer too.

And all this turmoil roiled, boiled and broiled throughout the kingdom of Max Amigo and at the next election he got blamed for the wall and everything else that was wrong in the kingdom. And through local, state, and national crooked elections, crooked without help from any foreign government one might add, it was assured that the now unpopular and hated Max Amigo was removed from office.

And during the whole time all this was happening, Don K. Haughty brayed, "See Max Amigo, I told you that you would pay."

"Remember class that such a wall actually existed once. Until Congress responded to the voice of all the downtrodden aliens in this country that is and took it down and opened the borders to freedom for the citizens of the world.

Does anyone know who Don Quixote was?" she asked.

No one responded.

"Oh well," she said and moved on to the next tale.

Chapter Twelve - The Business of Being King

There was a plague upon the kingdom. The subjects of His Royal Majesty the King were suffering from the lack of affordable health care coverage. They were getting little or no relief under the laws of the prior king whom the present King had deposed. So, His Majesty the King had called together a council of all the vassals of all the dukedoms, fiefdoms, and dumdoms that comprised his kingdom to remedy and replace the existing health care act with his own health care plan. The vassals all sat around the round table, for how else would one sit around a round table but to sit around it, with His Royal Majesty at the head of the table and wherever sat His Royal Majesty, that was the head of the table.

Each one of his vassals had his own plan as to how to save the kingdom and none of them were compatible with the King's. Thus, they all collectively defied the KIng rejecting his plan in its entirety. Thus, nothing was accomplished. All the while the people continued to suffer and die for lack of proper health care.

His Royal Majesty dismissed the lackeys with a flip of his wrist for he was a man of little patience and would not tolerate such foolishness and defiance. He had been a businessman in a former life before he became king. He was a man of action. A man who wanted to get things done. Done his way. Done now. So, he went to the Royal Magician and told him of his problem and commanded him to cast a spell upon the vassals and work his magic so that his healthcare plan would become the plan of the land.

The Royal Magician listened to the king, for that was all he was allowed to do, he was never allowed to question or contradict His Royal Majesty. But the King's plan was so complicated, convoluted and incomprehensible that the Royal Magician could not understand it. So, he asked for one asks and does not tell a king, the King, to write it all down on paper for him. His Royal Majesty did so. It came to only about a hundred pages. Quite a small number of pages compared to the twenty thousand pages plus law now in effect. His Royal Majesty believed in terseness not verboseness, keeping it simple for the simple folk.

The Royal Magician read His Majesty's plan, decided on a course of action, and then told the King how he would work his magic making the King's plan the law of the land.

"This is what I will do," he said. "I will take all the pages of your plan and cut them into little, tiny pieces. Then I will have the Royal Baker bake a huge, gigantic chocolate pie with all the little tiny pieces of paper in it. I will instruct him to make it extra chocolatey, extra gooey and extra sugary so that when the vassals eat it no man will know he is eating your words and find them distasteful. I will also have him mix in some special ingredients of sorcery magic, like toes of toad, silks of spiders, boils of bats, eye of newt, things like that, magic stuff. Then I will abracadabra it all with an ancient Druid chant and when the vassals eat the pie, they will ingest your words and the magic will make their tiny brains all think alike so that they will be all in agreement. In other words, they will regurgitate your plan and pass it."

"Brilliant!" exclaimed His Royal Majesty. "I hereby by royal proclamation, (an executive order that is), order you to do so."

So, the Royal Magician instructed the Royal Baker. And the Royal Baker began baking for after all that's what bakers do, they bake.

Now though the King approved of this magic plan, it did not go far enough as he was concerned. He hated those insolent fools who had dared oppose him, embarrassing him like that. They must pay for their insubordination. His Royal Majesty must have his revenge, hot or cold it mattered not. Thus, he came up with his own plan to supplement his prior one and spice it up so to speak.

Before he ascended to the throne, His Royal Majesty had promised to clean out the royal stables. The political horse manure there had been piling up for years and was beginning to stink. So true to his word, His Royal Majesty had started cleaning out the royal stables.

Then when no one was looking His Royal Majesty bagged up a couple of bags of horse droppings and hid them in the pockets of his royal robe. He then proceeded to the royal bakery and told the Royal Baker to take a break for he had been working too hard and to go outside and smoke a cigarette. The Royal Baker didn't smoke but he bummed a cigarette from a homeless person and pretended to smoke it for he dared not defy the King since the King could be a royal pain in the you know what sometimes.

Now His Royal Majesty would have his sweet taste of revenge against those who had not passed his law. He emptied the bags of horse droppings into the royal stirring pot containing the pie filling and stirred and stirred until all the horse droppings disintegrated and were completely mixed into the chocolatey gooey filling. Then he added even more chocolate and sugar to cover the taste of the droppings and stirred it in.

He then called back the Royal Baker. The Royal Baker returned the cigarette to the homeless person and finished his baking.

The King was in the Counting House counting out his money when it was time to open up the pie and for the birds to begin to sing.

So once again all the vassals gathered round the round table.

"I have had the Royal Baker bake a pie for you as a gesture of my goodwill and to show no hard feelings guys," the King announced. "Not a cherry pie but an extra rich gooey chocolate pie."

Oohs and ahs went up from the vassals.

"Now this time we are going to accomplish something. But before we do so everyone is to eat a piece of pie for that will be symbolic of us all coming together, passing a health care bill and giving us closure. Eat!" commanded His Royal Highness.

Everyone took a bite, then another, for the pie was quite delicious, extra sugary, and extra chocolatey as said and the lords could not resist its sweet taste. But His Royal Majesty did not take a bite for he was suddenly called away right then by the Queen he said.

The Queen who was in the parlor eating bread and honey and had not called him at all. It was all just a ruse and when the Royal Flunky at Arms informed the King that the pie had all been eaten His Royal Majesty returned.

He then presented his healthcare bill to the vassals and commanded them to sign it. But before they could do so they all became sick and had to trot out of the room for that is what they had, the trots. They never returned that day nor the next few days either.

His Royal Highness was flummoxed. He summoned the Royal Magician and demanded upon the pain of death to know why the magic didn't work. The Royal Magician panicked and told him that the Royal Baker must not have followed his instructions and not mixed up the filling properly. For if his magic formula is altered, even in the slightest degree, he told the King, then it would not work at all. It was the Royal Baker's fault, he said. So, His Majesty offed the head of the Royal Baker while covering his own tracks at the same time.

Well, all the vassals recovered. They recovered because they had previously passed a special health care just for themselves and the treatment they received thereunder led to a speedy and full recovery, the cost of which was charged to the royal treasury. But when they returned to work, they were just plain sick and tired of all this talk about health care. They found it distasteful and now decided to move on to something else like tax cuts for the wealthy, themselves that is. They decided that they would deal with health care later, like when the whole healthcare system collapsed, went into convulsions, and died a painful death. In the meantime, the people would just have to suffer.

His Royal Majesty sat on the throne. He was disgusted with this business of being king. Actually, he now realized it wasn't a business at all. It was politics, an unfamiliar mysterious thing to him. Not like a simple business deal that he could manipulate. He longed to be back in the business world and not in the world of politics where madness and stupidity ran rampant and nothing logical ever was accomplished. The more he thought about it the more he realized that he wasn't cut out for all this horse hockey. And he no longer could stand the agony of defeat. It was no longer good to be King. Thus, His Royal Majesty announced that he was resigning the kingship effectively immediately.

A public cheer went up from the masses and a silent one from the vassals. For after all it was their secret plan that had come together ousting the King from office. Every politician has a secret plan, just ask former King Nixon or King Wannabe Kerry. And don't you just love it when a plan comes together?

"Did you notice class how the nouns and verbs are, how shall I say it?" said Professor Hillary, "quite delicious."

The class politely laughed in response. They knew none of that ever happened. The story was just the wishful thinking of some people back then.

"Here is one more story about that legendary king, King Triumphant.

Chapter Thirteen - King Triumphant

There once was a kingdom called the United Kingdom of America that got a new king named King Triumphant. Before the new king became king, the kingdom was in the doldrums, to say the least. The economy was flat. No new jobs had been created for years and economic growth did not grow. It sagged, slumped, and sunk. The previous king had told his subjects that this was to be expected. That this was to be their way of life from now on and forever after and to accept it as normal. Normal that things would not get better. In other words, he told them, as politically politely and pretentiously as he possibly could postulate it, for them to shut up and live with it. But still pay your taxes, of course, so I can spend your money on social welfare programs to repay and prepay potential voters for our party the Demorats. For after all, the old king knew that elections had consequences and he would never ever let an election go to waste.

But alas the present election had gone to waste. A lesson that the old king learned most dearly when his party's candidate, Killary Kitten, the Duchess of Deceit, was not elected king. Well, actually elected royal person which was now p.c., p.c. standing for political censorship. For she had hoped to be the first female king and shatter and shard the paternalistic palatial palace plastered paneled ceiling. She cried foul when not elected and blamed it on the Plutonians from Plutonia. She told them that they had sent micro-radar nuclear wave messages into the voting machines throughout the land, programming them so that she lost and that her deranged dangerous demon of an opponent won. Why the Plutoniums would do such a thing she didn't make clear. In fact, she wanted it that way to be as clouded up as much as possible. She knew the drivel by media would have a field day with all this and it was a great way for them to expound their agenda, which was her agenda too of course. Then she went off and pouted in the spider webs of intrigue in the Tower of Deceit in self-pity exile in Clintonia. Clintonia having formerly been Clinton Ia.

Now new King Triumphant knew exactly what to do to fix everything for he had been a businessperson in his previous life before becoming king. He had built up a fortune far more greater, for he was in the black, than that of kingdom, which was in the red. He viewed his new kingdom as just another of his many businesses, ventures, or enterprises for him to play with. He knew he could bring it back from the baffling brink of ruinous ruination. He was looking forward to the challenge. "It's great to be great" was his campaign slogan that elevated him to power. And it was good to be king too.

So, the new king decided to cut taxes, not just for the rich but for everyone, for that was what democracy is all about, he espoused, treating everyone equal, rich or poor alike. No one should be penalized for earning more money than someone else and be taxed at a higher rate simply because they got it and can afford it. No, he was for the socialistic approach to taxation where all were taxed at the same equal rate for after all that's what his country was about, equality for the masses.

But there were some dukes in his kingdom that always opposed anything King Triumphant said or did. It didn't matter what it was for they objected to it just for the thrill of the high of objecting. Thus if King Triumphant was for it, they were against it. And they were against it because it always hurt working class families. Whether it hurt non-working class families they didn't say. And as to just how it hurt them, well they would be figure that out later. For as everyone knows a law has to be passed first so that one can read it and find out what's in it.

One such duke opposing King Triumphant's tax law was Duke Moonchild of the dukedom of Granola, the land of fruits and nuts. The new tax law was totally unacceptable to him and his subjects, he told the king. When the king asked him why this was so, his response was, "Because it is."

"Okay," said the king. "Can't argue with that. I hereby declare that the Dukedom of Granola is no longer subject to my new tax law. The old tax law will remain in place and your subjects will be taxed as they have been so taxed before." This was an executive royal order and though not exactly legal, Duke Moonchild was pleased with it and took it as law because he liked it.

Furthermore, he had shown his loyal leftists subjects that he had stood up to the royal rightist king and the king had blinked and backed down. Duke was the man now.

Duke Moonchild had his own aspirations to be king and hoped to depose the king through legal means, for that is how Duke Helter had come to power years ago, and not by regicide as some proposed. The 'some' quoted Shakespeare to justify this. The legal means here meaning with all due deliberate speed, by hook or by crook, by God, come hell or high water.

So, the tax rates stayed at the old higher rates for the citizens and corporations of the Dukedom of Granola and soon the subjects thereof wondered why they were being subjected to these higher taxes than the rest of the dukedoms in the UK of A. where the tax rates had been reduced considerably lower. So much so that the state tax rates of Granola were no longer sustainable for them, and everything had to be sustainable in Granola. They complained to Duke, but he did nothing for he was still reveling in his triumph over the king. So finally, when nothing was getting done, they voted with their feet and moved to a different dukedom like Heartlandia. And the Granola corporations moved too to Heartlandia.

To stop the flow of residents from his dukedom, Duke Moonchild cut Granola's state income tax rate. But he did so only a little for if he did too much then there would be no money for social welfare programs for the poor and downtrodden, and of course everyone wants to help the poor and downtrodden, and especially the underprivileged children of the poor and downtrodden. But alas he could do nothing about the United Kingdoms of America tax rates as issued by King Triumphant. So those with money, and those who wanted to keep more of their money, kept leaving Granola. And those without any money and on welfare program subsidies stayed for there was no point in moving to any other of the dukedoms of the U.K. of A anymore since there was full employment there and no government handouts of any kind to be had since poverty had been eliminated there.

Then the few wise people of Granola, over their duke's objections, petitioned the king to impose his tax bill on them too. But King Triumphant refused to do so.

"Elections have consequences," he told them.

But the real reason he didn't want to do so was that he wanted Granola to remain as a good example, a good example of a bad government. Things were going great, it's great to be great, for his Kingdom, and he did not wish not to impose upon his subjects a bailout of Granola. For it was a state he could not make great, again.

"Now the last story in this group ties together this president and all the others before him and emphasizes the solidarity of the office of president."

Chapter Fourteen - Rocky and Bullwinkle Discuss Their Presidents

Rocky and Bullwinkle were drinking at the bar at Moose Lodge #1313.

Bullwinkle said, "You know what I was just thinking about Rock?"

"You thinking Bullwinkle now, that's scary."   "I was thinking about all the presidents that we have lived through."

"Now that's really scary Bullwinkle. You're not going to talk about them, are you? I don't want to have flashbacks and relive all that. I don't know if I'll be able to take it."

But before Rocky could say anything further, Bullwinkle, now all wound up, started off on his tirade.

"First one I remember is Kennedy. No telling who he was screwing figuratively and literally to get himself killed. Then LBJ who didn't want to be the first president to lose a war so 50,000 American boys had to lose their lives so that wouldn't happen. Then Tricky Dicky, 'I am not a crook', Nixon. Yeah. Right dick. Then Ford, a total recall. Next Carter, pardon my French but what a 'oui nee wimpey', that means wimpy weenie in American Rock. Then Reagan and the contradicts and all that Oliver Stone stuff."

Bullwinkle then stopped, raised his hoof in the air signaling the bartender for another round.

"Don't get me worked up, Rock."

"You're working yourself up Bullwinkle. I don't have to do it for you."

Bullwinkle slammed down his beer, wiped his mouth with his hairy arm and continued.

"Oh, don't forget the Bushes. The first one, 'read my lips no new taxes', yeah right President Bush. And the second one, his mouth was his weapon of mass destruction too. And Clinton never had sex with that woman. Right. Presidents don't lie. Besides, that wasn't really sex anyway. And then Barama."

"It's Obama, Bullwinkle. Barack Hussein Obama"

"Yeah, yeah I know Balack Insane Obama. Did Obama care? Only about himself. Then came the Donald and he trumped them all now, didn't he?"

Bullwinkle took a swig of beer, wiped his mouth, and continued, "And as to Joe Biden. Well F____ Joe Biden."

"F____ Joe Biden?" echoed Rocky.

"Yah F____ Joe Biden Rock."

"And with that said the chant began throughout the Lodge, F____ Joe Biden."

Finally, the place quieted down. Some.

Bullwinkle then looked to the heavens as if he was in deep concentration and after contemplating something said, "You know Rock all these goofballs we've had as presidents and were still the greatest country in the world. It's beyond my limited brain power to figure it out. I just don't get it. Do you?"

"Yes, it's simple Bullwinkle. That's because all the other countries have worst goofballs than we do. Everybody knows that the best goofballs in the world are made right here in the good ole U.S. of A."

"I'll drink to that."

"Hallelujah and Amen to that brother," said Rocky as he chugged his Moosehead beer.

"Class, it is because of this last President they're talking about, and in light of his predecessors, that we have the laws that we have today that one must be certified sane before one is allowed to seek any office of any kind in this country and then again has to be certified sane before being sworn in and every thirty days thereafter." Professor Hillary had said the obvious. They already knew that because everyone today had to be certified sane every thirty days. This was to prevent many mass murders as well as single murders and to stop people from just going crazy in general. The congressional bill that enacted this was commonly called 'The Psychiatrists Retirement Fund Bill.

"Now the next couple stories will also deal with the election of that president who so much so changed our lives. These stories reflect the madness of that election but madness that we changed for the good. The first one is Fowl Election, then Barnyard Security, then Flippilocks And The Lost Election and finally A House Divided.

Chapter Fifteen - Fowl Election

Lucy Goosey was running for office, the office of representative of the fowl and stock on Farmer Dell's farm. Through the years she had been in politics continually and had stuck her beak in everybody's business and therefore deemed herself worthy of this job. But the truth of the matter was that she was just lumpy, dumpy, frumpy and grumpy. An old woman who had trouble waddling around the barnyard.

Her opponent was Cocky Red Rooster. He had never held any office before but felt himself qualified because he had clawed and scratched his way to the top of the pecking order. And besides, his comb was perfect. Perfectly kept in place all the time, never falling to the right or left, always standing straight up.

Farmer Dell would let the animals vote but he would count the ballots, or in other words pick the winner, for no way was he going to let the animals rule his farm. The election was just for show, to let the animals think that they had a say in things.

Lucy Goosey's co-campaign managers were Terry Bull and Penny Henny. She diversified her staff, half being fowl, half being beast, one a male, one a female, for it was the animal correct thing to do. One day when Famer Dell was out reaping the North Forty, she sneaked into his house and called her managers to discuss election strategy with them.

First, she spoke to Terry Bull. "We need to spread the rumor that Rooster never paid any taxes last year," she told him. "Everyone's got to pay taxes even if it's only chicken feed. Get on it," she ordered him knowing full well that Terry Bull would horribullize the rumor to the fullest extent possible.

She then gave Penny Henny the same instructions for she knew that Penny would run around like a chicken with her head cut off squawking, "Red Rooster pays no taxes. Red Rooster pays no taxes."

Farmer Dell lived a rural existence and thus his phone line was one of those on a party line. When the phone rang its shorts and long rings, it rang at the residence of each party member on the line, the call being intended for the party whose number of rings had just rung out, that is two short rings followed by a long, three short rings or whatever.

Myrtle Turtle was on the party line that Terry Bull was on and recognized the three short rings as a call for Terry Bull. She had no business picking up a call not for her, her ring was long short long, but she picked it up anyway, and listened in. She liked to listen in. She heard it all. Minutes later she also recognized the call to Penny Henny who was also on the same party line. She listened to that call too, for Myrtle Turtle was quite nosey even if she had a small one.

Myrtle had no vote in the election for she lived at the pond down the road. But she didn't like Lucy Goosey who always brought all those honking geese to her pond for their daily swim and gab sessions. She hated them because they were messy, always leaving goose feathers and goose crap everywhere. She knew if Lucy got elected, things would only get worse so she decided that she would use her new ill-gotten information to influence the election. She would sell it to Cocky Red Rooster so that he could use it to his advantage and get elected and she would get something of value from him in return. Rather than call him, for she knew that the line was not secure, she decided to walk to the farm and talk to Red Rooster in person. She got there a day and a half later and did so.

Cocky Red Rooster made a deal with Myrtle. He liked to make deals. It was the price to be paid for the info. So, he promised her that when elected he would see to it that no barnyard animals would ever again invade Myrtle Turtle's territory, that is, he would build her a fence around her pond.

Soon the rumor got out that Red Rooster had not paid any taxes and some animals believed it, but Red Rooster didn't care. He had a plan. He was a clever individual. He knew what to do. He did not deny the rumor and in fact proudly admitted that he had paid no income tax, though he actually had, and thereby he let the lie become the truth. He even crowed about it and promised that if elected he would teach everyone else how to do the same, so that they too could legally pay no income taxes. The voters then, rather than think that he had run afoul of the tax code, now admired him for outsmarting the government and flocked to his side.

Lucy Goosey knew that she fowled up. She knew that she had used an unsecured phone line and had thus shot herself in her own webbed foot.

And Farmer Dell knew what was going on too for he had his spies everywhere. He neither liked or trusted Lucy Goosey because she was so slick. Nothing ever stuck to her, just like water off a duck's back. And as to Cocky Red Rooster, well he was just plain repulsive to him. Always strutting around the barnyard like the cock of the walk or something. He had hoped that someone else would have run, someone like Sheri Sheep who he could have herded around without any trouble. These two would not do. So he asked his political advisor, his wife, what should he do.

"Well," said his wife. "It looks like Red Rooster is going to win and your sister and her family are coming over for Sunday dinner this Sunday. There's your answer."

"Huh?" said a nonplussed Farmer Dell.

"Like the song says. We'll kill the old red rooster when she comes."

"But what about Lucy Goosey? What do we do with her?"

"Christmas is only a few weeks away. All my relatives will be here for Christmas dinner. Goose is traditional at Christmas. Problem solved."

"Well, that was relatively easy," responded Farmer Dell. "Two birds with one's family stones."
Moral of the story: Politicians always foul up their nests.

The students were starting to get bored with all this political hogwash but to Professor Hillary this period of history was fascinating and she couldn't pull herself away from it for some reason or other. Thus, the next story.

Chapter Sixteen-Barnyard Security

The neighborhood watch committee was conducting an inquiry into the most recent carnivorists attack on the chicken coop on Farmer Dell's farm. Four eaten. No one came to the rescue and that was the reason for the inquiry, to find out who fouled up that night.

The first witness was Homer Homey, a homing pigeon, not a stool pigeon, though some believed him so, director of the FBI, the Fowl Bureau of Investigation.

Mr. Peter Peacock was Chairman of the committee, and this was his chance for him to strut his stuff like he did when taking selfies of his puffed-out tail feathers and sending them to young peahens to let them know that he was available.

"Now isn't it correct Mr. Homey," began Chairman Peacock, "that you have looked into this matter and found no evidence of any intent of wrongdoing by Lauralee Leghorn?"

"Yes, that is correct."

Lauralee Leghorn was the cluck hen who was on neighborhood watch duty the night of the carnevorist attack. Well actually Lauralee had determined that it wasn't an attack. Just a group, not an organized pack, of some indigenous meat eaters who had been watching a commercial for chicken wings on tv and got all worked up.

"Now the girls in the hen house tried to call Ms. Leghorn while the raid was taking place, but they got no response, did they?"

"Yes, that is correct."

That was because, as Lauralee Leghorn did her neighborhood watch rounds, she campaigned. She was running for President of Barnyard Security against Red Rooster, and she just couldn't bring herself to stop campaigning. Her time was too valuable to take calls.

"And isn't it true that Farmer Dell had given all the animals walkie talkies so that they could communicate with each other if there was any kind of a problem?"

"Yes, he gave them walkie talkies. He was too cheap to buy them cell phones."

"And isn't it true that there is a recording device on these walkie talkies that records everything?"

"Yes, and it doesn't allow for minutes to be erased. It was a new state of the art Anti-Nixon recording device."

"And you listened to that tape and found no evidence of any intent of any wrongdoing by Lauralee Leghorn, isn't that correct?"

"Yes, no reasonable persecutor would proceed with a case without evidence of intent."

"But now you say there is new evidence. Is that correct?"

"Yes."

"And why's that?"

"We have been provided some additional tapes."

"And do you have those tapes now Mr. Homey?"

"No, I do not."

"How come?"

They were given to me by one Rita Ratones and when she asked for them back, I was obligated to return them because they had not been subpoenaed."

"That's all for now Mr. Homey," said Chairman Peacock. "You're excused but don't fly the coop. You're subject to being recalled."

Homer Homey didn't fly away home. He flew up to the rafters and remained above it all.

"This Committee now calls Rita Ratones."

Rita Ratones scurried to the stand.

Rita Ratones had worked for Lauralee Leghorn and today she was going to rat her out her former boss in exchange for a permanent stay of execution for she had been convicted of the crime of verminity, that is being vermin on a continual and repeated basis and sentenced to death by rat trap next Tuesday.

"Ms. Ratones you found some additional tapes that you gave to Mr. Homer Homey, didn't you?"

"Yes," she squeaked.

Well, she hadn't exactly found them. She had taped everything her former boss had said and squirreled those tapes away for a rainy day, like today.

"And after Mr.Homey had listened to those tapes and announced that he found some new evidence on them you then asked for and got them back, didn't you?"

"Yes."

"Why did you want them back Ms. Ratones?"

Rita Ratones squirmed in her chair. "Ms. Leghorn told me to get them back or else Terry the Rat Terrier would be paying me a visit."

"But you didn't return them, did you?"

"No, I didn't."

"Why not?"

"Well after I got them back, I decided to keep them for my own personal security reasons and since I live next to the manure pile, I decided to hide them there because no one ever goes through manure looking for stuff. But the next morning before I got up Farmer Dell had already loaded up all the manure and spread it out on the south forty. So, I guess you can say the evidence has gone gone south, kind of"

The audience of feathered fowls cackled out a communal laugh.

Homer Homey then flew down to Chairman Peacock and whispered into his ear.

After a brief consultation Chairman Peacock announced, "I've just been informed that the FBI has been scratching, sifting, and poking its nose through all that manure trying to put the pieces of the tape back together again, and that the agents on the case are all highly qualified and trained having all graduated from the Humpty Dumpty School of Evidentiary Science. Ms. Ratones, you're excused for now."

Rita Ratones squirmed out of her chair and ran down the nearest rat hole.

"This committee is adjourned until tomorrow morning at which time it will then recall Mr. Homer Homey to give us an update on all the manure he's been through."

But the committee never did reconvene. Homer Homey was nowhere to be found. Some said he had flown the coop. Others said Famer Dell had squab for supper that evening.

And as for Lauralee Leghorn, well she didn't get elected. Red Rooster did and he promised to get to the bottom of all this right after he took office. But he never took office. Farmer Dell's relatives were coming round the mountain for dinner next Sunday and they killed the old Red Rooster when they came.

Professor Hillary quickly skipped over this fable for it gave women a bad name and moved on to the next one.

Chapter Seventeen - Flippilocks and The Lost Election

There once was a young girl named Flippilocks. She was named that because her golden curly hair flipped up at the ends and bounced happily up and down as she went about her studies at one of the best self-proclaimed liberal arts schools in the country. Besides she flipped out easily and often and the name kind of fit.

And it came to pass that an election was held in the fall of her senior year and that her candidate lost. She could not deal with that and true to form she wigged or flipped out as they say. This was because the results were not to her liking, not the results she had been promised by the media and the pollsters.

She had been given counseling by the university, at taxpayers expense of course, to readjust her to the realities of the world. But alas nothing worked, and she became so frustrated and discombobulated that she could not concentrate on her studies and would not graduate next spring because she failed some of her courses.

So, she thought, what does one do when things aren't to one's liking in this country? Why one sues someone of course. So, she hired Attorney Oyster Shyster, a man with pearly white teeth, though that was not the reason she hired him. She hired him because he would take her case on a contingency fee basis, one third of whatever she got. She had no cash for an attorney because her student loans had bankrupted her for the rest of her life and a contingency fee was the only way she could hire an attorney. But she wasn't wanting money, though Shyster was, really, she was filing suit because it was the principle of the thing and nobody sues unless it's for the principle of the thing. Right? That principle here was that one of her constitutional rights had been violated, the right to the pursuit of happiness. No way could she ever be happy with the person elected as President for he was not her president. The system had done her wrong.

Oyster Shyster, ever the attorney, decided to sue the one with the deep pockets here, the Federal Government of course. And not it was not just the Federal Government and its system of electing a president that had done her wrong, others were to blame too. So, he sued both political parties, one of them had to be to blame, but he didn't know which one, so he sued them both, and all the pollsters for having lied to her. They had all ruined her perfect life.

Attorney Miles Mole represented all the defendants. They only needed one attorney because basically they were all just one big entity anyway and were in cahoots together as usual. He was a shrew of a shrewd little man with a scrunched-up face, squinty eyes, and two sharp buck teeth. He had spent a lifetime tunneling in and out and through the legal system and he knew all of its intricacies thereof and therefore he knew he was doomed to lose this case.

This was because the case was brought before the Supreme Court, a court of supreme, or should it be said extreme, principals and or principles. The case had been fast tracked to the Supreme Court at their request for they deemed it of national importance and urgency.

And so, the trial commenced. "Mr. Shyster," began Chief Justice Rue Unhingedburg, "you are asking the court to void the election and award a trillion dollars in damages to your client. Is that correct?"

"Yes, Your Supremeness," Oyster Shyster answered knowing that if he got a trillion dollars damages, his fee being one third thereof, he couldn't do the math in his head, but he thought it had to be in the millions, and that therefore he'd probably get enough money to retire on.

"A trillion dollars?" asked the black guy on the court.

"Yes, Your Supremester. You've read the report of our psychiatrist Dr. Seigheil Freund which says that my poor client will never be cured. She will need constant psychiatric attention. Even if she has a good election and is healed, any bad election will cause her to go into a relapse arrest. It's kind of like having shingles you know Your Honor. You're never cured. My client will have a lifetime of medical bills and a trillion dollars would help some in paying those bills." Oyster Shyster paused for effect and pointed to his client. This was Flippilock's cue. She put on her sweet sad forlorn pouting cute little face and looked soulfully and sorrowfully as she batted her big blue eyes at each justice one at a time. "There see her. See how she suffers," proclaimed Oyster.

"Objection," spoke up Mr. Mole. "This child is covered under her parents' insurance until she is twenty-six thanks to the Amazing Health Care Act. She personally incurs no medical expenses at this time. Her folks do."

"Good point," said the black guy.

"But not good enough," retorted Justice Unhingedburg. "There's no point in coming back to this court asking for damages at a later time when we can award them now. Judicial efficiency is important," she said not knowing she had just created a new oxymoron. "Knowing that there's unlimited money for her in the future will help put her mind at ease now, today. Objection overruled."

"Thank you Most Exalted One," said Shyster as dollar signs flashed through the caverns of his mind. "Your Honor at this time the Plaintiff calls the Plaintiff Miss Flippilocks to the stand."

"Objection this is highly unusual Ms Justice, witnesses testifying before the Supreme Court," interjected Mr. Mole.

"Well, this election was highly unusual too wasn't it Mr. Mole? Objection overruled. Proceed Mr. Shyster."

Fliipilocks pranced up to the stand, her golden locks bouncing as she went. She curtsied to Justice Unhingedburg, took the oath, but promised to affirm as to the truth and not to swear to it, for a proper young lady does not swear, sat down and fluffed out her red, white, and blue colored fancy laced dress, her attorney picked it out for her to wear today, and smiled her cute dimples at the court.

"Now tell us how this election ruined your life young lady," asked Attorney Shyster.

"Well," she said, and here she paused, her brow furrowed. The windmills of her mind were not winding or milling as she tried to think of an answer. Finally the best she could come up with was, "Well, it's just not fair that's all."

Oyster Shyster knew he wasn't dealing with the most honed knife in the drawer, and she might not cut the mustard as a witness, so he took charge. "And it's not fair because the media and pollsters promised you that your candidate would win, didn't they?"

"Yes."

And it's not fair because the president elect hates women, will hold women back from realizing their full potential and thus you or all other women everywhere will never ever be able to crash into the glass ceiling, will you?"

"Yes."

"And it's not fair because he will make you pay for your own birth control pills and you're afraid as a result thereof of that you will get pregnant and have to spend a lifetime raising a bunch of children you didn't want, aren't you?"

"Yes."

"And you're worried that he will step up the war against women and take away the right of women to vote and to drive cars, aren't you?"

"Yes."

Justice Unhingedburg got caught up in the excitement of this line of questioning and jumped right in, "And you're worried about the rights of millions of Americans to receive welfare, and of the deportation of millions of lawful poor Mexicans and their families, and of moving the Berlin Wall to the Mexican border, and of spending billions of dollars on the military rather than helping the downtrodden citizens of this country who are victims of an unfair system of discrimination aren't you?"

"Your Madameness I don't know what all that means. I just know that I want my life to be like it was before all this happened, when everything was just right." She lowered her head, took out her white embroidered dainty hankie from her made in American designer pocket book and wiped away forced tears from her rosy red cheeks.

"I don't believe that's asking for too much Your Honor," piped up Oyster Shyster. "Politicians promise to make it right for us all the time."

"Point well taken Mr. Shyster," applauded Justice Unhingedburg. "Your witness Mr. Mole."

Mr. Mole scrunched up his little face and waited until Flippilocks was through wiping away her fake tears. "Ms Flippi, excuse me Ms. Flippilocks, "You've never had a job, have you?"

"No, I haven't."

"And your folks have taken care of their little girl, meaning you, all your life, haven't they?"

"Well, yes."

"So, if they created you, and they cared for you, then they, not the government, are responsible for taking care of you now aren't they?"

"Good point," said the black guy.

"No, it's not," barked Justice Unhingedburg, "Everyone knows It takes a government. That's an old African proverb. You of all people black guy should know that."

Miles Mole knew he was doomed.

Oyster Shyster had gotten out his calculator and was starting to figure up how many millions a third of a trillion was.

Fliipilocks sat there waiting for the next question from Attorney Shyster, but he was so absorbed calculating his fee that he forgot all about her. She wasn't used to being ignored. She was used to being the center of attention and after a while she couldn't hold it in anymore and she imploded, "I just want to be happy. Is there anything wrong with that Your Godliness?" And she started to weep.

"Nothing is wrong with that dear," responded Justice Unhingedburg. "You have the constitutional right in this country to the pursuit of happiness and it's this court's responsibility and duty to see that this right is not denied you. An election cannot trump your right to happiness." Justice Unhingedburg went over and put her arm around the now sobbing young woman.

So, the court ruled that day that the election would be set aside because it was too upsetting to poor Flippilocks and had prevented her from exercising her right to the pursuit of happiness. And it further ruled that a new election was to be held and what the results therefrom were to be, based on the previous popular vote of course.

As to damages, well the court dared not increase the national debt by another trillion dollars because that would not be the politically prudent thing to do. So that they denied.

Mr. Shyster couldn't retire, not quite yet anyway.

And as to Mr. Mole he went back to the darkness of his office and buried himself in his files and law books for the brilliance of the court's ruling not only hurt his eyes but his head too.

And as to Flippilocks, well, she didn't understand what had happened here, but she read on the internet somewhere that she had won and that made her happy again.

Professor Hillary discussed this story to a great extent. She liked it. She liked the next one too.

Chapter Eighteen - A House Divided

The inscrutable Judge Kangarito sat on the bench today. Today was landlord-tenant day. In other words, it was the day that the tenants got kicked out of the apartment or the house that they were renting for lack of paying rent. Of course, they all would have some standard excuse why they couldn't pay and why they shouldn't be kicked out. Like their landlord was a rotten awful person who never took care of the place and wouldn't fix the things that they told him needed fixing and therefore they didn't have to pay any rent until such time as all those things were fixed to their personal satisfaction. But this next case Judge Kangarito could see was not going to be a standard case because the defendant was the President and he claimed that he had a right to stay on in the White House and the plaintiff was the President Elect, or so he thought he was, who wanted in the White House now, since the President was technically a dead duck anyway and had no business wasting this country's precious time with stupid executive orders and pardons for criminals.

Ram Emanuel Sheep represented the President. He was a headstrong and fearless attorney who had a reputation for butting heads with anybody and everybody. He never failed to get his point across, sometimes both of them. Though this was a civil case, and he was a friend of the President, his fee was being paid by the taxpayers.

Mr. President Elect was represented by a bevy of expensively suited attorneys, some of which were even minority oriented or women, and all of them had the word esq., esquire that is, after their name. That meant that they were honorable people. Mr. President Elect bore the cost of this army, but he could afford it since he was ten times richer than the President. Besides all of this was tax deductible anyway.

Judge Kangarito began. "Mr. Sheep you're claiming that what we have here is a tenancy at will when it comes to who may reside in the White House. Is that correct?"

"Yes, your honor. The occupant of the White House is there at the will of the people. That is why it's a tenancy at will. No rent is paid, whether monthly or yearly, no lease is signed, for any period of time, and therefore the occupant thereof is a tenant at will of the landlord and the landlord here is the people, or should I say the will of the people. And even a tenant at will is entitled to a written notice to vacate and none has been given here because it is the will of the people that he should stay."

"What say you, one of you attorneys for Mr. President Elect?" asked Judge Kangarito.

One of the minions rose. He was a giant of a man, a former NFL linebacker, who loved to tackle things head on. "Your Honor the people here have given written notice through the electoral college. The law has been complied with. The defense should be penalized for delay of game." He couldn't resist throwing some sports jargon into this. After all, if he just went out there, played his game, stuck to his game plan and did what he had to do, he could win this thing. But then he added, thinking to cover all bases, even though he was not a baseball player, "The President should be ordered to vacate with all deliberate speed." He used the phrase" with all deliberate speed" because he had read that once in a Supreme Court case somewhere and thought that it would impress Judge Kangarito if he threw in some legalese. He sauntered over to his chair, John Wayne style, gave a thumbs up to his client, and plopped down, a smirky smile upon his face.

"Mr. Sheep your response."

"Your Honor the electoral college is not the will of the people. It's the will of the electoral college. They are two entirely different things. The will of the people is reflected in the polls and here the polls show that it is the will of the people that my client stays. They further reflect that my client could have beaten Mr. President Elect on a level playing field, if the deck hadn't been hacked and stacked against him by foreign foes, which is what happened here of course. Furthermore, they show him more popular than the president-elect and also more popular than his worthy female opponent. In fact, they show him even more popular than the two of them combined. That is the will of the people."

The linebacker blitzed. "Your Honor everyone knows that it's the Democrats who have hacked into the polls and altered the results to their liking. Why this has even been reported in some newspapers, and you know newspapers wouldn't report something if someone had not said it. Besides, polls are hearsay and inadmissible."

Ram Emanuel Sheep consulted with the smartest man in America, his client. The President remembered something about the fairness doctrine from when he taught constitutional law, but he wasn't quite sure if constitutional law applied here or not. Nevertheless, he gave Ram a one minute summary thereof, a summary to the best of his recollection that is.

"Under the fairness doctrine, Your Honor, it's not fair that the will of the people be denied," spoke up attorney Sheep. "Under the fairness doctrine, what is fair is that everyone's a winner, and that includes my client. This is one of the very first things that we teach our kids in school today, that everyone in this great country of ours, is a winner. And the reason for that is because we don't want any poor child's psyche to get damaged and their life become ruined and need repair if they have to worry about losing. No child should ever face the possibility of being a loser. Incidentally treatment for this, if it should so happen, heaven forbid, is covered for free under the Amazing Health Care Act." He couldn't resist getting this plug in. "Why if the President should lose here today, this could upset his children and we can't have that now can we? How would you like it if your father was a loser?" Ram Emanuel Sheep sat down confident that he had butted his opponent on his keister with that bit about the children. Always play the children card. After all, no one wants to hurt innocent children.

The swarm of the President Elect's attorneys were all abuzz. Then one emerged from the hive and made a beeline to the bench. It was not the linebacker. This attorney was a former Victoria's Secret model who had that extremely rare combination of beauty and brains, and she was dressed somewhat differently than the other attorneys.

"No one here is suggesting that we hurt or abuse young innocent children Your Honor," she said standing in front of him, with her two top buttons of her blouse unbuttoned, as she looked up and batted her eyes at the judge as he fixated on her fluffy blouse. "But if anybody's guilty of abuse here, it's the Defendant for abusing the judicial system, abusing executive orders, abusing Congress and above all abusing the American voters. Please keep in mind your honor that under the fairness doctrine the majority shall not run rampant, shall not run amuck, shall not destroy the minority."

"Nor the minority over the majority," bleated Mr. Ram Emanuel Sheep.

The Victoria's Secret attorney walked back to her table. Walked back in the way that she had been trained to walk down the runway, kind of sashaying from side to side as she went. Not another word was said until she sat down, then Mr. President Elect himself spoke up. "Your Honor if we could take a short recess here perhaps the parties here could make a deal and get this settled."

"No way, your Honor. Polls have consequences and we have the pollsters to prove it," baa-ed attorney Sheep.

"Will take a fifteen-minute break and if a dee-ar," Judge Kangarito was trying to say deal, "hasn't been made, I'rr (I'll) give you my ruring (ruling)." Judge Kangarito was still having trouble pronouncing his el's as he was a recent immigrant from Japan via Syria since Syria was the quickest way to get into the country now thanks to a recent executive order.

Judge Kangarito was a political appointee, not that there's anything wrong with that, after all that's how one gets to be a judge, through politics, and therefore he knew what side his sushi wasn't buttered on. But above all he knew he had to appear fair and non-political, so the press didn't tear him limb from limb and eat him alive. So, after he had finished his tea and read his tea bag, he re-entered the courtroom and made his ruling, this time pronouncing his el's correctly.

"I have heard the arguments of counsel and both sides have made some good points." Always praise both sides. That was one of the first things that they taught you at judge school. That way their clients will feel they're getting

123

their money's worth from their attorneys. He continued, "I'm going to apply the law of the Bible here," He dared not quote the Koran, for though the President might appreciate it, he still had to go with Christianity since the latest polls showed it still the dominant religion in this country, as of last week anyway. "And apply the law of the wise King Solomon. In other words, I'm going to split the baby. Therefore, the President shall reside in the left wing of the White House and Mr. President Elect shall reside in the right wing. The President shall remain the president of the blue states and Mr. President Elect shall become the president of the red states. I am aware that President Lincoln once said, 'A house divided cannot stand. That it must either become one or the other.' But things are different today. Today no one should have to have a president that they don't want, a president that is not their president, a president that they cannot identify with. There's no reason here why everyone should not be a winner. Mr. Lincoln was not infallible. He was a president, not a judge. So be it. The house is divided."

Both tables were abuzz now. The Defendant was happy because he got to stay on as president of a people that he could easily manipulate and furthermore he could ban any opposition now by executive order. And the Plaintiff was happy because he had gotten rid of those blankety blank blue states. The blue states were just troublemakers anyway and this way he wouldn't have to make any deals with those jerks.

The judge had made a good ruling. Everyone was a winner.

Professor Hillary just couldn't seem to get enough of this presidential election stuff and in her excitement, she had forgotten all about something called collusion back then and how it figured into all this. Though the fable was not presidential election material it still had collusion in it and that was good enough for her. She would figure out later how to tie it all together, So she had them read The Curse of Collusion which follows.

Chapter Nineteen - The Curse of Collusion

The High Commissioner of baseball was one Cooey Mountaintop Boone. She was a delicate dove of a damsel who sat atop the wonderful world of baseball, America's most treasured, beloved, and hallowed pastime. It was her job to decide what was in the best interests of baseball whenever any controversy came up so that baseball would not soil itself. For as said she was a dove of a woman and could not allow herself or baseball to be soiled. Today such a controversy was before her now. The Cubans had colluded and thrown the world series. In other words, they rigged it. Shades of 1919 only worse, much much worse, because this time politics were involved.

Her decision had long been a foregone conclusion of collusion as far as Her Eminence was concerned. Only the formality of an impartial hearing remained in order to show the world how fair and just she was in dealing with such a travesty.

The culprit here was one Duriel Muriel, a Cuban national playing for Houston, and yes Houston did have a problem. It seems that Senior Muriel made an insensitive gesture by slanting both his eyes with his fingers and then pointing to one Yu No Who, the opposing pitcher who was of Korean descent. (Well at least we knew who wasn't on first).

He was represented at this hearing by one Flea Bailey, an attorney who volunteered his services wherever he saw an injustice being done anywhere in the world like now. This crazed crusader of justice knew that his client was doomed and didn't stand a politician's chance at Heaven of having a fair hearing here today. His only defense was to jihad all this and take down as much of baseball with him as possible. Or in other, more American words that is, take as many of the enemy to Hell with him like they did at the Alamo while trying not to come out looking as bad as Custer did at Little Bighorn.

Ms. Boone was both prosecutor and judge here and she was out for bear. "Take the stand Senior Muriel por favor," she growled at him in her best Spanish accent.

Senior Muriel took the stand. The ritual began.

"Well?" she roared to the doomed accused.

"Well, what?" Muriel meekly responded. Attorney Bailey had coached him in acting meekly.

"Well, what do you have to say for yourself?"

"There was something in my eyes and I was just rubbing my eyes, that's all."

"Don't pitch me that bull. Everyone knows that was a very insensitive thing for you to do. Don't you know that it's against the law in this country to be insensitive, offend people, and hurt people's feelings. You're not in Cuba anymore Senior Muriel where you communist people have no feelings for each other like we do here in America."

Muriel bowed his head in fake shame, shaking it from side to side soulfully. Bailey gave him two thumbs up review.

"You got anything you want to ask him Mr. Bailey?"

"Yes, Your Eminence."

"Well make it quick then."

Mr. Bailey began his kamikaze defense.

"After you rubbed your eyes, you weren't pointing to the pitcher then, were you?"

"No, I was not."

"Who then?"

"Who then was I pointing to?"

"Yah who?

"Yahoo?"

"No who."

"Well it wasn't Who. That's who."

"Who was it then?"

"Enough with the schtick already," bellowed Her Correctness.

"It was Israel Ishmael."

"Israel Ishmael the Cuban outfielder for the Trolley Dodgers. Is that who you were pointing to?" The Trolley Dodgers was the original name of this team that bleeds blue blood.

"Yes."

"And why?"

"No, I wasn't pointing to Senior Why. He's not Cuban." Duriel was referring to Bill Why, the second base guy of the Trolley Dodgers. "I was letting Israel know I had put the Voodoo Cuban Curveball Curse on his team."

"What?" asked a flabbergasted attorney Bailey, taken back in fake shock while putting his hand over his heart, opening his mouth, and bugging out his eyes. "What?" he repeated again in an over-emoted, likewise astonished response. The bad acting award was his for the taking.

"Watt? I didn't do it to Senior Jay Jay Watt." The Jay Jay came out Hay Hay in Spanish. No one dared laugh though for fear of offending the entire Hispanic culture. Jay Jay Watt was the Trolley Dodgers first baseman. (When someone asked who's on first, the answer was, of course, Watt's his name.)

129

"Forget the who, why, and what of it Duriel and just tell us how come you did it."

"I was just following orders. That's all," he said in his best non-German accented voice.

"Orders from your man in Havana?"

"Yes, from our man in Havana."

"You mean your and Israel's man in Havana?"

"Yes."

"And when you were making all those signs to him like touching your nose, your cap, your ear, crossing your chest, they weren't baseball signals like a manager or base coach makes were they?

"No. They were my orders in code."

"And what exactly were you signaling him?"

"I told him that I had put the Voodoo Cuban Curveball Curse on them as ordered and that he too should do likewise just to make sure the curse worked. And he signaled back to me that he already done so."

"So," continued attorney Bailey excitedly, "One could say that you two, Senior Ishmael and yourself, that is, were in cahoots, or cahoosion, or collusion to fix the game then. Is that correct?"

"Yes, one could say that if one wanted to say that," answered Duriel as he bowed his head in fake shame, laying it on the chopping block of justice.

The room went deathly silent.

"Your Eminence I hereby hand you a dossier that I have composed," exclaimed attorney Bailey, and he had in fact himself composed it, "of all the Cuban infiltration into baseball from the minor leagues all the way up to the majors. How the Cubans have infiltrated the minor league farm system and how they plan to take over Major League Baseball and socialize it. Why there are things in here you wouldn't believe." And that was true. There were things in there designed to rock and shock and blow up the baseball world. Some of that stuff that he made up was truly unbelievable, but now that politics had been injected, like it was into everything else in this country today, the unbelievable became the believable.

Commissioner Boone began thumbing through this top, self-created, secret document. Her jaw dropped. Her eyes widened as she read a couple more pages and then announced, "We'll take a break now while I review this in my office and then I'll come back and give you my decision."

Bailey let out a sigh of relief and patted his client on the shoulder.

Shortly thereafter Her Eminence herself seated herself upon her throne and she herself announced her ruling.

"As all of you know it is my job here to rule in favor of the best interests of baseball. Baseball is and always has been holy in this great country of ours, the country of its origin, the mecca of its sacred birth. The U. S. Supreme Court has ruled many many years ago that baseball is exempt from the antitrust laws and that baseball is a game and not a business. Therefore, baseball is free to make its own rules and regulations. So based on that foundation I rule, and again all in the best interests of baseball, as follows:

First, I order the dossier of Attorney Bailey be impounded and sealed until such time as it may be ruled otherwise by myself or my successor."

She could not have the contents revealed as it was much too much a hot political potato to serve the press. Baseball would implode if the contents became known to the public.

"I am doing this because I find collusion or cahoosion, take your pick, here between the Cuban baseball players and the Cuban government to monopolize and take control of baseball, in other words a conspiracy. Therefore, I further order Mr. Bailey to turn over the entire contents of his office and his computer immediately to Major League Baseball and place him, his client, and Israel Ishmael under a gag order not to talk about all this on pain of lifetime banishment from baseball.

Second. I am ordering Seniors Muriel and Ishmael to remove the Voodoo Cuban Curveball Curse from baseball effective immediately, again on pain of a lifetime banishment from baseball if they don't do so. Once this is done, they can remain in baseball subject to the terms and conditions of a parole that I will later so harshly impose upon them.

Thirdly, I am issuing a travel ban on all Cubans either coming into or going out of this country until further order. Furthermore, I am extending it to any Venezuelans also because of all the Venezuelan players in the league as I find that their government is in cahoots with Cuba.

Fourth: I am ordering a Congressional Committee be impaneled and chosen by myself to get to the bottom of all this." The crud had already risen to the top.The Committee would skim it all off though.

"Fifth. As to Senior Muriel's insensitivity to Papa San Who." The Commissioner was a little confused on the use of this term Papa San. "I am ruling that even if I believe the Defendant's cock-eyed concocted story about just rubbing his eyes, I still find that he was grossly negligent in doing so and therefore I assess him a fine equal to one tenth of his annual salary to be paid instanter to Major League Baseball." She wasn't sure just exactly what that number was, but she knew it had to be in the tens of thousands of dollars. She figured that since most churches in this country wanted a tenth of your income that this figure had to be fair.

"This is my ruling. So be it," she decreed. "This matter is hereby adjourned."

Attorney Bailey slapped his client on the back and smiled a smirky smile.

"Gracias," said Duriel, thankful that he hadn't been deported or sent to Guantanamo.

"De nada," said Bailey. Attorney Bailey had done all this pro bono but the publicity from it was worth a fortune to him in future fees. His threat of a jihad defense to blow up baseball was a success thanks to the confusion of collusion or cahoosion or contusion or whatever it was called.

Who says terrorism doesn't work? Not Who that's who. (Sorry couldn't resist.)

"What you should take away from this story class," said Professor Hillary, "is that sports are just like politics. They had political teams just like sports teams back then and it was win or die. Count your lucky stars all that changed, and we have only one party today, the right party. Avoids a lot of hassle and bitter feelings for us all that way.

Now as to the next two assignments to read, well they just don't fit in anywhere, but they're important as they show how the criminal legal system worked back then and how the courts dealt with the issue of race. The first fable is about Willie Weasel, a criminal.

Chapter Twenty - The Sentencing of Willie Weasel

Miles Mole represented the State, Rosie Robin represented the Defendant and Judge Kangarito presided over the sentencing of one Willie Weasel.

Miles Mole was a little shrew of a man with a scrunched-up face and squinty eyes. Nevertheless, he had seen it all in his years as prosecutor and nothing got by him.

Rosie Robin was a chirpy young thing who viewed herself the champion of the downtrodden. She had little experience trying cases but she more than made up for that with her zealous enthusiasm.

Judge Kangarito was an inscrutable occidental having been appointed to the bench because of his ethnicity. Therefore, he always made sure that he never ever exhibited any specie bias.

And Willie Weasel, well Willie Weasel was a sleaze, a wily character, always smarter than the Pigs, until they caught him that is, which they always did. Given more chances to straighten up and fly right than there are of winning the lottery, he figured to be released from the cage today and slink away as usual.

"Since the Defendant has been found guilty, is everyone ready to proceed on the matter of sentencing?" asked Judge Kangarito.

"Yes, Your Honor." came back the chorused response of the two attorneys.

"You may proceed Miss Robin."

"Thank you, your honor."

Miles Mole perked up. Even he couldn't help but notice her pretty red breast which she made a point of flaunting before the Judge. Her legs were spindly though and she was a round robin. Her overall appearance was that of an apple on two popsicle sticks.

"My client was raised by a single mom," she woefully began. "He had no father."

"Objection your honor. He had a father obviously or he wouldn't be here. He just doesn't know who he is, which I might add, is par for his kind." Miles had gotten her on a technicality.

So, she rephrased. "There was no father for him to turn to in times of need when he was growing up. His mother had a hard time of it raising four cute little kits without any help. She did the best she could in a high crime neighborhood and was a victim of crime herself when one of her babies was eaten by a feral cat. This was the environment in which poor Willie Weasel grew up, an environment of crime and poverty.

"Enough already with the violins Your Honor. She's tugging at my heart strings with this sad epic tale of woe. Can we move on please before bailiff Bird here has to start handing out kleenex."

"Get to the meat of the matter Miss Robin."

"Yes, Your Honor. Our defense here is that Mr. Weasel is an underprivileged animal. He never had a chance in this dog-eat-dog world of the survival of the richest and the fittest. The odds were stacked against him the moment he was conceived because all the other animals are prenatally prejudiced against him."

136

"Objection Your Honor. Being underprivileged is not a legal defense and besides weasels are born weasley not underprivileged. Their genetic DNA makeup makes them what they are, criminals. And her client's got a rap sheet as long as my arm to prove it."

Judge Kangarito chuckled. "You sure you don't want to retract that last statement Mr. Mole. Your arms aren't that long you know,"

Rosie Robin moved her left wing over her lips to hide her smile and Miles Mole buried his face in a case book as he tunneled back to his table.

Judge Kangarito continued, "In any event Mr. Mole is correct Miss Robin the law does not recognize 'underprivileged' as a legal defense. However, the law does recognize the defense of over privileged, that is when one has been raised in such a way, with so many privileges, that one does not know right from wrong. Do you have anything to present to this court as to your client being overprivileged?"

"Yes, Your Honor."

"Objection Your Honor. Miss Robin has already said that her client is an underprivileged animal. He can't be both underprivileged and overprivileged at the same time. Besides there's been no evidence that he never learned right from wrong."

Rosy Robin had no idea how to proceed when she said, "Yes, Your Honor". She had just said it reflexively. But now it came to her, thanks to Mr. Mole. She was going to stab Miles Mole in the back with his own objection.

"Your Honor Mr. Mole is correct in that one cannot be both underprivileged and over privileged at the same time. But one can be both at different times, which is the case here. First as a child Mr. Weasel was under-privileged. This led to his criminal behavior. Then because of his being underprivileged the courts felt sorry for him and placed him on probation, suspended his sentences, ordered community service etc. etc. time after time. In society's attempts to assuage its guilt for its prejudices, it was in reality over privileging Mr. Weasel, making him what he is today."

Rosie Robin paused to catch her breath. She was on a roll now and proud of herself for her quick thinking. So she continued, "Like I said he was over privileged. And because of all this Mr. Weasel doesn't know right from wrong anymore. Consequences become meaningless to him. He's not responsible anymore for his behavior, not because of his nature, as Mr. Mole here would have us believe, but because of his nurture, his nurturing by society. He's the victim here. The system has done him wrong." And with that elegant condemnation of the legal system Rosie Robin ended her oratory and sat down triumphantly for she had stuck it to Miles Mole and had championed the downtrodden at the same time.

"Mr. Mole, what say you?"

"Judge since Mr. Weasel doesn't know right from wrong anymore, and since society made him what he is, then the least that society can do for him is to unmake him. Unmake him from what he is, into what he should be. Your Honor Mr. Weasel suffers from mental disabilities not of his own making as Miss Robin has so kindly pointed out for us. He has psychological problems that need to be treated, not only for the best interests of Mr. Weasel himself, but also for the good of society, and therefore a prison sentence would not be in everyone's best interest. No, your Honor, no prison for Mr. Weasel. Mr. Weasel should be placed in an institution where he can receive the help he needs and be confined there until such time that he is fit to rejoin the rest of us. That is my recommendation Your Honor." Mr. Mole scooched himself back to his table hoping that Judge

Kangarito would take his recommendation which would in reality be a life sentence for someone like Weasel because, as they say, you can't change the spots on a leopard. He wanted to add "How you like them worms Miss Robin," but thought better of it.

"What speak you, Miss Robin?"

Rosie was stymied, fumbled her legal pad and stammered "Could I have a moment to confer with my client your honor?"

"Please do Miss Robin."

Rosie was confused. Miles Mole had manipulated the roulette wheel of justice on her to make it look like he was the winner here. But why had he done so? She didn't know and she didn't know what to say to her client. But that was okay with Willie Weasel because he spoke first.

"I'm taking the nut house deal."

"You're what?" She asked fearful that her client didn't know what he was doing.

"I'm taking the nut house deal. Be there six months at the most. Hell, it'll take them longer to do all the goddamn paperwork on me than the time that it'll take for the doctors to cure me."

"You sure you want to do that?"

"Yeah I'm sure." He wanted to say, "Look lady, I've been around the barnyard a few times. I just didn't crawl out of my hole. I know how the game is played. I know how to game the system. I can con those quack doctors there into believing that they have cured me." He wanted to say all that, but he didn't. He was smart enough to keep his mouth shut. So instead, he smirked, "Six months tops and I fly away free from the cuckoo's nest. Tell the judge I'll take mole face's deal."

So, she began her spin. "Your Honor, my client feels from the bottom of his heart that he needs treatment and therefore we ask the court to place him in an animal hospital for the criminally ill until such time as the vets there find him cured." Miss Robin felt comfortable now relaying this, since that was what her client wanted and since it made her look good because he got no prison time.

"So be it. Miss Robins please prepare an order to that effect, have Mr. Mole approve it, and present it to me for my signature. Court's adjourned."

Both attorneys left the courtroom that day believing that they had got the better part of the deal. Miss Robins because her client didn't get prison time and Mr. Mole because her client didn't get prison time. No, instead Mr. Weasel got a life sentence as far as Miles Mole was concerned. Born a criminal. Stay a criminal. Stay a criminal forever in a mental institution for the criminally ill.

And Willie Weasel left there a happy soul too, believing that he had beaten the system one more time.

"Piece of cake," bragged Willie to Bailiff Bird as Bird led him away.

"Yeah, you're a piece of work alright Weasel," responded Bird.

Everyone was a winner that day. That's how the justice system works.

"The criminally ill are no longer a problem now class as you already know," commented Professor Hillary. "Thanks to universal mandatory certification of saneness. This story reflects this so be sure to remember it at test time class since we are almost at the end of the term now. Our next story will deal with the matter of race. Please read The Court of Ridiculous Claims and Thank God we're all just one race today, the human race."

She failed to mention that something like one to four percent of the human race still carried Neanderthal genes.

Chapter Twenty-One - The Court of Ridiculous Claims

The Court of Ridiculous Claims was in session. Mr. Jett White, the plaintiff, who was black, was represented by Miss Lily Black who was white. The Defendant was the good ole USofA. and proudly represented by Ms. Grey who was neither white nor black, nor gray for that matter either, but a red, white, and true blue blooded feral American. But she wore a gray pants suit though. The case was one, kind of one anyway, for reparations. Or in other words how much one could get for having ancestors that were slaves.

The judge was Max Brown. He was not black or white or gray but kind of brown, but not Hispanic brown but Jewish brown. He was a shrewish trollish looking little creature who had to sit on a couple of thick old musty law books in order to peer his scrunched up old face out over the bench. With wrinkled up nose and furled brow he glared down upon the litigants through his coke bottom bottle glasses. He was pretty much blind but then again justice was blind, just like love was blind. His oversized ears protruded from his bald head, bald that is except for a little dusty gray around the edges, at right angles which was good because he was hard of hearing and needed to take in as much direct sound as possible in order to catch the drift of a conversation.

"Miss White let me get this straight," Judge Brown harrumphed. "Your client is claiming that his great grandfather was born a slave in 1862 and never got his forty acres and a mule when the slaves were emancipated because he was a minor at that time. Is that correct?"

"Yes, your honor. And we are asking for the value of those forty acres and a mule, which were the reparations at that time, in today's money of course as compounded for over one hundred and fifty years or in other words somewhere between eight and eighteen million dollars. Whatever the court deems fair and just Your Honor."

"Eighteen thousand huh?" responded the judge. "What say you Ms. Grey?"

"Your Honor the statute of limitations has long expired. Mr. White's great grandfather had two years after he became twenty-one to file for his acreage and mule and never did so. The claim is therefore barred. There's no way they're entitled to eight thousand dollars." She said eight thousand, quite loudly for the judge to hear for she knew the judge was going to award something because after all this was the court of ridiculous claims. So therefore, a ridiculous lower number was better than a ridiculously high number as far as she was concerned. She only hoped the judge would remember it. "No way is he entitled to eight thousand dollars," she repeated again quite loudly.

"Eight thousand huh? What say you, Miss Black?"

"That is all beside the point your honor. One of the last executive orders out of our former president's mouth was to give wronged, victimized, traumatized American citizens, wronged victimized and traumatized due to slavery that is, the right to sue for reparations. The statute of limitations was abolished, abolished quite clearly I might add, in that order." She handed the judge a certified copy of the executive order as she spoke. The judge took it, looked at it, but it was all a blur to him, so he nodded affirmatively and handed it back to her.

"They got you on that one Ms. Grey," he hollered. "Continue Miss Black."

The plaintiff then proceeded to introduce into evidence all sorts of ancient probate records of the deceased slave owner who owned Mr. White's ancestor. Mr. White's ancestor was listed in the inventory of that estate and that along with a complete genealogy chart tracing him from then to now and Mr. White was enough to prove beyond a reasonable doubt that Mr. White was the only living direct descendant and therefore entitled to as much as he could get.

"Now as to our second claim," said Miss Black. "We will prove that my client is entitled to tons of money because the Emancipation Proclamation was an illegal act. We will prove that the freeing of the slaves, without proper congressional authority, was a taking of my client's other ancestor's property all without due process of law and therefore without just compensation, and that my client is the sole living descendant of that ancestor and therefore entitled to lots more money. Entitled to the money that his ancestor should have gotten in the first place when his property, his slaves were taken from him by freeing them, but didn't. Furthermore, it should be compounded and magnified to reflect current day value."

"Excuse me Miss Black, but are you saying your client's ancestors owned slaves, a black man owned slaves?" asked Judge Brown dumbfounded.

"No Your Honor, this ancestor was white and we will prove, again beyond a reasonable doubt, a direct genealogical connection from him to the Plaintiff." And

143

again, through probate records the Plaintiff proved that the deceased ancestor fathered a child by one of the hundreds of slaves he owned at the time of the Emancipation Proclamation. And Plaintiff further proved value through probate estate inventory records of the time assessing his slave's worth in dollars. And further proved through current actuarial tables that in today's figures, these slaves, which were personal property once, would have a value of eight point eight million dollars.

Ms. Grey sat there fascinated by all the historical proof, but she was ready when the Plaintiff rested. "Your Honor as the Plaintiff has so clearly pointed out for all of us to see, is that President Lincoln actually, in reality, in effect, issued an executive order when he freed the slaves. He did it without congressional approval and therefore voila it had to legally be an executive order. Furthermore, there was no provision for compensation in it. First the Plaintiff wants money because of an executive order and then second, he wants money even though the executive order did not provide for it like the first one did, i.e. forty acres and a mule. He can't have it both ways, Your Honor. Live by the executive order, die by the executive order." Ms. Grey sat down quite smug proud of herself for having thrown this executive order nonsense back in her opponent's face.

"What say you, Miss Black?"

"Sure, he can have it both ways, Your Honor. After all the Government has things both ways, their way, all the time, and the people are the government, and my client is one of the people. One of the little people out there, one of those little people that always keep fighting for their rights, one of those little people who are always downtrodden and that have been taken advantage of by the evils of big government. He's just one of the many little people out there, Your Honor. But you can't keep the little people down forever. No sir for they will always rise up like David of the Bible and smite that Goliath of injustice, the federal government." And here Mis Black paused and sighed and went over and put her hand on her client's shoulder and with her other hand wiped away a tear. "And therefore, since the government can have it both ways Your Honor, they should get it stuck to them both ways."

Miss Black smirked at Ms Grey. Ms Grey lowered her eyes and looked at the floor. Judge Brown harrumphed again for good measure while Mr. White leaned back in his chair, his hands clasped together behind his head, put his feet up on the table and grinned Cheshire cat style from ear to ear.

Miss Black continued; she was on a roll. "The color of one's ancestors should not deny one's claim for justice. Black or white should not deny one the right to the green to which they are entitled."

Ms. Grey interrupted, "Your Honor there was a great American who once said that he had a dream that the day would come when a man, and if he was alive today would say a man or a woman, would be judged not by the color of their skin but by the content of their character. Here Plaintiff's claim has no redeeming content, no redeeming character. It has nothing to do with color. It's just a grab for money as the Plaintiff has admitted."

"What say you Miss Black to logic such as that." Judge Brown had been waiting for the race counter race card to be played as it made things fair and balanced and spared him from having to invoke it.

"That's my point exactly Judge," she responded. "The only color that matters in this country is the color of money. Money to be given to one not on the basis of that person's color but on the basis of the color of justice and the color of justice here is green. The Emancipation Proclamation was a taking of property without compensation. Money is due."

"Judge," said Ms Grey. "Even if you don't think it was an executive order back then because executive orders are a recent phenomenon allowing congress to pass on their responsibilities and duties to the executive so that they don't have to make decisions and be held accountable for doing anything, you still cannot invalidate the Emancipation Proclamation. To do so would be un-American." Then she had an epiphany and said, "Do not press down upon the brow of America this thorny crown of racial guilt. Do not crucify America on a cross of paper money." Ms. Grey knew she had read something like that somewhere before, but she couldn't for the life of her remember where, but what the heck she gave it a shot anyway. It sounded kind of good.

"Doesn't make any difference what she says Your Honor," countered Miss Black. "The law can be applied ipso facto nunc pro tunc." She threw in this legal mumbo jumbo as one always looked intelligent and learned if one spoke some Latin while palavering in the language of the law.

Ms. Grey remained silent. She knew she was behind the eight ball. It was only a question of which way the decision was going to go, an award ridiculously high or an award ridiculously low. "Eight thousand dollars at the most Judge," she repeated.

Judge Max Brown had heard enough. He had been maxed out so to speak. Everyone, including himself, was thoroughly confused. But that was good because it made the case look very complicated and difficult and thus any decision would appear to have been rendered in deep thought and would ooze lots of judicial thinking. The ridiculous thing to do here of course was either to award an outrageous sum or deny the claims in their entirety, either way would be extreme and in keeping with the spirit of this court. But the judge liked to split the baby so to speak, for that too can be ridiculous. In other words, let each side win some and lose some. That way it looked like he had put some thought into his decision and the attorneys could each claim a slight win for their record book. But in reality it was ridiculous because when everyone wins no one wins. So he allowed the first claim and awarded the Plaintiff the equivalent of forty acres and a mule in today's value of four hundred forty four thousand four hundred forty four dollars and forty four cents and denied the second claim citing something about ex post facto, e pluribus unum and quid pro quo, which of course made no sense at all.

So much for that case he thought as the parties left the courtroom. Tomorrow's should be more exciting. He would get to decide who gets the money for selling baby parts, the state, the abortionist, or Planned Abortion Hood, and oh yeah maybe even the mother and he better not forget the father. He may have rights too.

The semester was coming to an end now and Professor Hillary had saved the last two stories for now.

"The final two stories are about students. Not students just like you but about students back then in the early twenty first century. Both stories are based on true incidents but have been enlightened somewhat to make for a good fairy tale read. The first is Hungering for Justice and the second Dreaming of Diversity. Both deal with social issues of the day that weighed heavily on the minds of students back then. Enjoy.

Chapter Twenty-Two - Hungering for Justice.

There once was a young college student who attended one of those Ivy league schools. He was one of the best and the brightest of his generation and that was a fact because his school had told him so. "Whoever shall goeth to our school is among the brightest and best of this generation," the university proudly proclaimed and drilled this into his ever expanding still adolescent baby brain. And he believed them for he craved to be among the elite and the future leaders of this great country of ours.

Now being a college student, he was under a traditional obligation to protest. This obligation he gladly accepted for he was hungry to bring justice to all and to change the way things were done in his country. But what to protest against? There were so many things wrong here. So many things to protest against. So, he used his brilliant mind and thought and thought about it and decided to protest against the government. A government that he didn't vote for, that was not his government, and would not meet his personal wishes, concerns, and demands. Had this ever been done before he asked himself?

And then he remembered from his history studies when college students many many eons ago had protested against a government that they did not like, and how they brought down a president that they did not like. Perhaps he could do the same here. Perhaps history can repeat itself after all and not doom us all in the process while doing so he thought.

So thus encouraged, his encouragement soon overflowed. His mind was going a mile a minute now, for that is the speed at which brilliant minds work, a mile a minute. And he thought but why stop here?" Why not protest against everything. If you're going to do something, do it whole hog. He was sure of his reasoning now. Sure, that he was right and sure that he should go ahead. Go ahead and protest against all the injustices that his country had committed past, present and future, for surely, they would listen to someone as smart as him and from such a prestigious school too.

So, he made a list of an number of things that were worthwhile protesting against which included among other things the old standbys, racial injustice, profiling, obscene corporate profits, pipelines, coal, fracking, guns, closing of the borders, sexism, cruelty to animals, death penalty, global warming, child abuse, etc. etc. etc. ad nauseum. And he wrote them up a multi page manifesto spelling it all out as to where he stood on each issue and how the government should correct these injustices. His plan was to release his manifesto to the drive by media when they were driving by in the neighborhood. Of course, many of these things had been protested for years and years and had been done to death, and in fact were becoming quite boring to the public, but he was not discouraged in the least for the times they were a-changing just like they always did.

He hit upon the idea of a hunger strike as a way of protesting against the government and announced to the mainstream media that he was on one. The media loved this kind of hokum and soon were begging him for interviews, and he ate it all up, even if he was on a hunger strike. But soon he realized that this hunger strike business was not as easy as he had thought it to be, for he became in fact hungry and craved something from the four basic food groups of college students, pizza, snacks which included beef jerky and twinkies, light beer, and wings. And after missing a couple of meals he could no longer bear the hunger pains. So, he decided to take it upon himself and change the rules of hunger striking, nunc pro tunc, (That's latin for now for then. He was pre-law of course) so as to make it easier for him to hunger strike while at the same time still getting his point across. Thus now one could eat when one became hungry because after all that's what a hunger strike was all about, being hungry. And each time he became hungry, well that was the government's fault, not his, for if they had met his demands, he wouldn't have become hungry and wouldn't have had to have eaten after all if they had. This all made perfect sense to him. Another way of 'striking' a blow against injustice everywhere. He was proud of himself.

This continued for some time, the press eating it up. And soon people and organizations with a political agenda brought him food. And each time they did so, they feasted on the publicity.

Now with plenty of food he was eating three full meals a day as well as snacking every couple of hours in between to tide him over to the next meal. And all this having to eat because he was hungry just proved over and over again that his demands for justice had not been met and that his strike was a success.

Well, the young student began to gain weight and when one reporter asked him how the hunger strike was going he responded, "Real good I gained five pounds last week."

This eating when you're hungry hunger strike went on for some time and the young student's weight ballooned up to three hundred pounds and he developed diabetes and other obesity related health problems and he called for his doctor.

But alas, he was not allowed to have his own doctor and he was told by the governmental authorities of the governmental health care program that the government would give him a number and put him on a waiting list for a government approved doctor.

The strike went on and on and after a number of years the young, now old, student's number was up. No not his number in line waiting for a government doctor but literally his number was up. He died, poor soul, from all the complications of his hunger strike still hungering for justice but not for anything else.

"That actually happened class," Professor Hillary informed them. "No, he didn't die but that's how he conducted his hunger strike, by eating when hungry, and when you think about it, it makes perfect sense."

Just for the record Professor Hillary was a graduate of the same university as the hunger striker.

"Now read the last story and we'll discuss it tomorrow. Remember it's a true story that happened in Illinois. (That great Democrat state.)

Chapter Twenty-Three - Dreaming of Diversity

Justin and Dustin were identical twins. They were not diverse. They were a couple of cards. Not aces, but some of the other students at the university called them something like that beginning with the letter 'a'. Actually, they were a pair of jokers. The attended Feinstein University a school named after some feminist of the early 1900's. But the twins couldn't care less who it was named after, for they, in the fashion of the typical male college student there, referred fondly to their school as F.U. They thought that was funny.

Now the twins and the other students sat in the main auditorium. Every so often they were forced to attend some goofy lecture or program of some kind or another and today was one of those days. So the two of them sat there absentmindedly as the speaker of the day droned on and on.

True to traditions of the school and in keeping in tune with the old and the new, some ultra-extremist feminist student at the university had come up with a brilliant idea, endorsed enthusiastically by the university of course, that she wished to present to the student body. So, she informed her fellow students that she had conceived of a project combining diversity and the women's movement, since this was women's history month, and that it was in the best interests of everyone, both male or female, to participate.

153

For they all needed to be exposed to both diversity and women's history, that is, for their own spiritual health and well-being she told them. Besides that, she hinted that this was going to be a cool thing to do. Cool always worked with students or they wouldn't buy it.

"Diversity is what brings us all together and that's what this country is all about," she proudly proclaimed from high on her soapbox on center stage.

Justin and Dustin picked up bits and pieces as she droned on. They had been having trouble staying awake. Finally, somehow they put it all together and it registered in their still developing young male minds, for men's brains and maturity develop slower than women's and that's why women have an advantage over men, that there might be a chance for playful mischief to be had here. They stifled their guffawing and snickering best they could for a while and then one of them suddenly burst out, "Oh that's what this country is all about is it? Not anything else huh? What about football, basketball, sports? Isn't this country about that too?"

Then the other one quickly chipped in, "and beer."

"Typical men," the speaker shouted back, trying to blow them off best she could. But she was hardly heard over the ongoing laughter mainly from the disrespectful, as to be expected, male students.

When things quieted down somewhat, she continued, "Ms. Monica Manley our head librarian has so graciously allowed us to conduct this project in her library this being Women's History Month."

"When's men's history month?" shouted one of the twins.

The speaker again glared in the direction from which the taunt came unable to determine who said it. She couldn't control herself and rose to the bait. "You dumb men are history as far as us women are concerned."

The twins each had their own comebacks ready but decided the wiser thing to do would be to keep quiet as a couple of school officials on the stage rose from their chairs and started scanning the audience for the culprits. The twins were men, but they weren't Neanderthal men.

Ms. Manley, short of stature, stepped forward and stood up on the soapbox. She was wearing her grey pants suit uniform that she always wore. It matched her gray bobbed gray hair. She looked down at the student body through her rimless granny glasses. That she was a homely woman goes without saying. And with that said, she began.

"What we are going to do students is this. We are going to have you students take naps in the library and when you wake up you are going to write down the dreams that you just had about diversity and/or women. You will then post your dreams on the bulletin board for all of us to read so that we all can see the different diverse ways we look at diversity and/or women while in a subconscious state and so that we all can have adult intelligent conversations and discussions concerning the same. Signing your name to your dream is optional. To encourage diversity and appreciation of diversity and of women's rights, we have displayed posters concerning both all over the library to help stimulate you in your dreaming. Pleasant dreams and thank you." With that said Ms. Manley sat down to a weak round of applause.

"This will be a hoot Bro," said Justin to Dustin. Or was it Dustin to Justin?

"Ya, I can't wait to dream about women."

"Ya, that's all you do. Just dream about them."

"Ya, dream about getting it on with different, oh excuse me diverse, women. That's want I want to dream about, diversifying women if you get my meaning. I'm getting stimulated just thinking about it."

"I'm going to 'read' Playboy before I go to sleep to self 'stimulate' myself," said the other one, whoever he was.

"They don't have Playboy in the library. It's banned Bro. It's sexist. Guess you'll just have to settle for National Geographic and look at pictures of emaciated bare breasted women from third world countries instead."

So, the boys decided to participate in this 'experiment' or 'project' or whatever it was. They couldn't pass up this chance for them to be their own creative snarky selves. They prided themselves on that. They couldn't let this opportunity go to waste. So one sat down in a chair and pretended to sleep and the other put his head down on a library table and faked sleep.

"Pssst," said one to the other. "You dreaming?"

"Ya, I'm dreaming, daydreaming, daydreaming about all the diverse women I'm going to be doing. What about you?"

"I been thinking about what we should write after we're done napping. I think instead of posting two manly dreams we should post one manly one and one not so manly as in keeping with the theme of diversity you know."

"You mean like we write about one dream from a manly point of view and one like from a womanly point of view."

"Exactamundo and we both sign the manly one and say since we're identical twins we have the same brain wave lengths and dream the same things. Ms Manley and those women libber chicks will probably buy all that since they think all us men think alike anyway."

"And the other dream?"

"The other we write from a gay womanly point of view praising the virtues of diverse gay women. And we sign that one Monica,"

"Monica like in Monica Lewdinsky?"

"No Monica in like Monica Manley. Ms. Manley's first name is Monica. Didn't you hear that when the speaker introduced her?"

"I must have been sleeping then."

So the boys report of their joint mutual manly dream was as follows: "Dreamt about women, white ones, black ones, brown ones, red ones, and yellow ones and how we made a connection with each, if you get our drift, and how we enriched our mental and physical, with the emphasis on the physical, well beings and souls. Diverse women are kind of like the spice of life you know. Like the old nursery rhyme says: little girls are made of sugar and spice and everything nice. We enjoyed this project and hope to repeat it often. Thank you for letting us share our dreams." Signed Dustin and Justin.

"There that ought to roil up their hormones but good," said one to the other as he pinned it to the bulletin board.

"Whose? The men's or the women's?"

"Both."

"Now here's what the one by Ms. Monica will say, " said the other twin. "I dreamt I was flying on a big goose across the heavens. Flying all over the world meeting, greeting and conversing with and sharing the goals of our sisters in Europe, Africa, South America and Asia. Touching their hearts and minds, melding with their souls, and all of us expressing ourselves as true universal women. A dream that I hope to see come true someday. Maybe not in my lifetime because there is still much left to do in the fight for equality but someday, we will all come together and have closure."

"What the hell does all that mean anyway? And what's with the goose?"

"How the hell do I know what it means? It just sounds good and uses lots of things people say nowadays when talking about stuff like this. As for the goose, duh look at the poster on the wall behind you dude. The Adventures of Nils Holgersson. See him riding a goose. It's by some Swedish feminist dead gay woman who wrote children's books years ago. This is women's history month you know so who else would Ms. Monica dream about but one of her heroes, excuse me, heroines."

One of the twins, whoever it was, wrote it up as such and signed it, Monica. He had a copy of her handwriting before him, and he did a fair job as a forger.

The results of their dreams were posted and though many of the others posted were just as gross and ridiculous in their own way as Dustin's and Justin's, theirs was immediately denounced as male chauvinistic swine nonsense and taken down and shredded, burning violated fire code, by the feminist library control assistants as the twins called them.

But as to the one signed by 'Monica,' it was highly praised and the students fawningly congratulated Ms. Manley, as if one can congratulate one for a dream, for sharing her enlightening dream.

Ms. Manley never told them that the dream was not hers because she could not let all this academic enthusiasm go to waste. Even though she suspected who wrote it, she would not ruin the moment for the students and divulge the truth. And she emphasized to the students, mainly female but some metro male students as well, that the power of suggestion of the poster was important here because it caused people to subconsciously think a certain way and therefore more women's movement posters should be placed around the campus.

As to Dustin and Justin, well they weren't there when all this was going on. They were at a kegger each looking for a woman. They had only one criterion when looking for women and it wasn't diversity. For they were desperate men.

Upon reading this story no student could believe that male students actually acted like that back then. All that silliness had been bred out of and or programmed out of today's males thanks to the scientists of feminism. For today's students' sexism no longer existed and thus there were no longer any campus date rapes. Today's students all lived happily together in their perfect world of coed dorms. Their perfect world that they had been taught to appreciate from day one in the public school systems.

"Now Class," announced Professor Hillary, "our next class will be our last and I'm giving you a rather large assignment to read. It's one more story as to the failed court system of the times. It's a novelle or novelleter or whatever they called it back then about a fellow named Caper Kallenbach. It's Kafkaesque or Orwellina, take your pick or choose both for that matter. It's not in your book so I'm handing it out," she announced as she began distributing the story. The students took it back to their dorms and read it.

Twenty First Century American Fairy Tales
B. Craig Grafton

Chapter Twenty-Four - The Political Correctness Trial of Caper Kallenbach

Once upon a time, and not that long ago, there lived a citizen by the name of Caper Kallenbach who lived in the KIngdom of Trumptopia. He was an aging, early sixties, white male of a nondescript description in that he looked like a lot of other white old males his age. He was bland, generic, not much to look at, had a paunch, love handles, crow lines under his eyes, and some grey hair remaining around his ears but not enough for even a tacky comb over. However, he had enough hair at the back of his head to tie up into a ponytail and wore it that way tied up in a red bandana. He stood, well more like slumped, at about six feet for he had been six foot in his youth but had shrunk some in his old age. His weight, well, hadn't shrunk. He hadn't dared looked at a scale in years because he didn't want to know his exact poundage. Nevertheless, just from looking at him, one would classify him as slightly, but not grossly, overweight. And as to his complexion he was as lily white Anglo-Saxony as they come. He had blue-grey eyes with bags under them of course. He was old and worn out and knew it and it bothered him that he couldn't do anything about it. He knew his time here on earth was about to come to an end and sometimes he wished he had lived his life differently.

He had been married once but that didn't work out and after fifteen years and two kids later the marriage ended in divorce and he became a free man again. Back in the days of his youth, when anyone over thirty was considered old, Caper figured that his fifteen years of marriage was half his lifetime down the drain. He never remarried and prided himself in the fact that he never made that mistake again, marrying that is.

He had been a working man all his life, though he had gone to college in his youth but never graduated. Didn't keep his grades up. Got caught up in the antiwar movement back then protesting and demonstrating against the war, against the government, against this and that, against whatever they had to protest against back then. Protesting took up so much of his time that he neglected his studies and didn't pass his courses. He flunked out of school. Thus, he lost his student deferment and was expelled from college.

The question before him then was, 'Ask not what your country can do for you but what you can do for your country?' And his country had the answer to that question for him, fight communism, and he was drafted into the U.S. army. First he did time at an army training concentration camp called Fort Leonard Wood in the heartland of America and then he did time at a place now known as Ho Chi Minh City in the apocalyptic heartland of darkness. Luckily for him he never saw combat there for he knew if he had, he would not have been able to deal with it and would have had a mental breakdown. Knew that he would have ended up in a cement cinder block VA hospital somewhere bouncing off the white walls in a white padded rubber suit, not getting the help he needed, and kept on a short leash chained like a mad dog for the rest of his life. Maybe even put to sleep, through an accidental death of some kind, in order to reduce the government's hospital costs for he had heard stories to that effect. Even now all these years he still had recurring dreams about his time in uniform and they never went away. They were constant reminders of how he had blown or thrown his life away. He blamed the government for doing this to him. But he also blamed himself for letting himself get trapped by a government that forces its citizens to do things they don't want to do, and this still haunted him to this very day.

When he got out of the service the times, they had been a changing. The answers no longer blew in the wind for him. The war had ground to a halt some fifty thousand some American boys' lives later and all was quiet again on the western front of civilization. He was a different individual now after the war, a beaten individual, an individual who now blended into the scenery not to be noticed by anyone, and especially not noticed by his government, and that's the way he liked it.

He had gotten a job, one that didn't require a college degree, because he had a wife and a kid to support after he did his gig in the army. Got a job in the proverbial widget factory. In fact, that was the name of the company he worked for, The Proverbial Widget Company and he worked there for thirty some years before retiring last year. Did piecework making widgets, whatever they are, and was a devoted, if not rabid, union activist, for some of the old spirit of activism still burned in the belly of his heart. He became a union steward and enjoyed fighting for his union. The job was an eight-hour shift on his feet all day and it had caused him back problems all his life. But he toughed it out in order to get his retirement benefits for after all he really had no choice. He never was able to set aside any additional money for retirement. The bills just kept rolling in and just like millions of others in the entitlement kingdom he counted on his retirement pension and social security to get him by in his rusting, not golden, years.

Now today he was taking his two grandchildren, Noah age eleven, and Emmie aged eight, to see a professional football game here in his hometown. Caper was a big Bruins fan and today they were playing their archrival nemesis the Minnesota Norsemen. He had only the two grandchildren, his son's children. His daughter was a career businesswoman with a college degree that had cost him a fortune. She had chosen not to marry. She had chosen not to have a husband or a family. She had chosen a lifetime of devotion to her career instead. Caper admired and respected her for that, doing what she wanted to do, for in his youth he had marched with, among others, the women's movement for the right of women to do exactly that and he was proud of himself for doing that then and proud of his daughter now.

Caper loved his grandchildren dearly and like all good grandparents doted on them constantly. They were good grandchildren, obeyed him, minded their manners, respected their elders, good students, and good athletes even at their young age. Just ask him. He'd tell you. He went to all their ball games and cheered them on as if the fate of their little worlds depended on the outcome, which it did, to them anyway. And just like everybody else's grandchildren his grandchildren were perfect too. And if you don't believe that all grandchildren are perfect, just ask any grandparent, if you have an hour or more of time to kill, and they'll be more than glad to tell you about their perfect grandchildren.

He found their seats, got the kids the candy and soda they wanted, a beer for himself, and they all settled in now waiting for the game to begin listening to the buzzing of the crowd as people swarmed in like bees, beelining it to their seats.

The signal for the game to begin came, as it always did, with the blaring announcement of the faceless public address system announcer. A bellowing voice, it was always a male voice, with an Orwellian overtone and undertow to it, that made the announcement, cold, solemn, and stern like. "And now ladies and gentlemen would you all," all was the key word here," please rise for our national anthem." It was understood by all that this was not a request but a command. That everyone was to rise, without exception, and reverently sing along. Hand over heart being optional, so far that is anyway.

His grandchildren rose for they had been taught in school to rise and recite daily the pledge of allegiance with your right hand, never your left for whatever that meant, over your heart. This came naturally, almost pavlovian, to them now. So they stood there straight as an Native American arrow, their little right hands over their little hearts, God bless them, and sang along. They knew the words of course having been indoctrinated with them in the public school system, day after day.

But not everyone rose that day. Everyone except for a bunch of, that means quite a lot of, gaudily tattooed black football players. Caper called them blacks even though now they were now known as African Americans. He grew up with the word black for that is what African Americans called themselves, in a black is beautiful sort of way, back in the day. His folks grew up with the word 'colored' and used it because even coloreds back then called themselves colored. But now all this phraseology had morphed into African Americans. And it was the African American football players who refused to show their flag the courtesy, the respect, it demanded of them.

But those bunch of African American football players were not the only ones who didn't rise that day. Caper Kallenbach didn't rise either, the only white person in the whole entire stadium who didn't do so. Now Caper didn't remain seated to show solidarity with these players, solidarity another contemporary coolterm, no he did so because of his recurring back problems. Every so often his back would start acting up and start hurting him again like it did today. He first noticed it on the way here to the stadium while driving and knew he would have to schedule another visit with the chiropractor next week. The chiro couldn't permanently fix his back problem caused by being on his feet all day for years at the widget factory, he could only give him temporary relief which is what Caper desperately needed now. The pain was becoming excruciating. Getting up and down only made it worse and if he sat still and didn't move, the pain would eventually go away. So, he sat there not singing along. He just sat there and respectfully cast his eyes upon Old Glory.

"Grandpa get up," pleaded Emmie tugging on his shirt sleeve. "You're supposed to get up."

His granddaughter was to the right of him, and he looked up at her and said, "Grandpa's back's acting up today, Sweetie. It hurts for me to get up and down." That was as polite as he could put it for it hurt like hell whenever he got up and down. Then he remembered, his memory was going some, that he had some pain pills in his pocket that his doctor had prescribed for him whenever he couldn't stand the pain anymore, like now. So, he started to reach for them by sticking his hand in his pocket and as he did so he squirmed in his seat causing himself even more pain. He eventually dug them out with his right hand. In his left hand was his cup of beer and he was about to pop the pills into his mouth and wash them down with a swig of beer when the man next to him on his left glared down at him and said, "Get up." Didn't say 'Please get up,' but just a harsh command, "Get up.'

Caper ignored him and popped the two pills into his mouth and took a big gulp of beer.

"Get up." This time the command came with a growl in it.

Caper looked up at him and noticed the man was about his age and this was confirmed from the baseball cap that he wore the front of which read, 'Vietnam Veteran.'

"Get up before I help you up," the vet directed in no uncertain terms.

There was no doubt about it to Caper from the way the man said 'help' that he meant 'I'll drag you up,' and not that I will be so kind as to assist you in rising if you are not able to do so yourself.

Caper politely but firmly responded, "Please mind your own business, sir."

Now the veteran had seen Caper take those two pain pills and put two and two together and saw what he believed was an old hippie. He came to that convoluted conclusion based on the following. Caper had a ponytail, had a red bandana handkerchief tied across his forehead, wore a brightly colored tie dye T-shirt, faded blue jeans held up by a big black belt with silver rounded beads embedded in it and a big silver buckle that said something he could not read, it actually said something about Caper's union, and he wore sandals a la hippie style with his white socks. Clothes made the man and evidently to this veteran these clothes made Caper a hippie man. Besides, the man was popping pills like hippies do to get high.

"Show some respect for your flag and your country man," hollered the veteran over the communal singing of the crowd, "before I have to make you."

Personally, Caper could take it or leave it, showing respect for your country that is. Today was quite different than when he was a youth he had little, if any, respect for his country. But now in old age he had mellowed somewhat and did love his country and especially the president of his country. As for this man next to him though Caper had no respect at all because he was telling him what to do and Caper instinctively did not like to be told what to do by anyone. He sat there and ignored the ever becoming more so disgruntled agitated veteran.

"Hey, let go of me man," said Caper as the vet started tugging his sleeve.

This torqued the veteran off even more for it confirmed that this man next to him was actually a hippie. That's how hippies talked. Every other word they used was 'man'. Not only did this fool not respect his country and flag, but he did also not respect him as a veteran, a man who had put his life on the line for this great country of ours. He had done so, just like Caper had by being drafted, but he kept that to himself, and that didn't matter anyway as far as the Vietnam vet was concerned. He roared over the singing, "I fought for this country. What you do? You and your hippie 'buds' burn down some buildings on campus back in the day. Riot in the streets." He reached down and grabbed Caper with both his arms and attempted to pull him to his feet. Caper anchored himself in place by grabbing his arm rest with both hands having spilled his beer all over himself when he did so.

Caper was glued in place. The veteran was determined on ungluing him. Caper was set on standing, his ground that is, by sitting. That comment about hippies brought flashbacks to Caper and he thought back to what he stood for and stood against things back then. He had lost all that enthusiasm for any cause years ago when he got trapped into a job, marriage, and a family. Again, it came to him that life had passed him, passed him by in the blink of an eye, and it was time to do something about it. Time to do something about it now in the few remaining years of his life.

"Get your hands off me or I'll have you charged with assault," screamed Caper. He had had enough. He had reached his breaking point with this man and this flag reverence business. Why should I stand, he thought. There's no law that says I have to stand for the flag, have to stand for anything, physically or mentally. "Get 'em off me," he screamed again as the veteran still kept trying to hoist an anchored Caper to his feet, "or I'll have you arrested."

"I'll have you arrested," shouted back the veteran.

In all the excitement neither man had noticed that the anthem singing was over and everyone had sat down except them. The two of them were causing a scene and a security person noticed this and hurried to them.

"What's going on here?" she asked. The security person was a woman. No way could she, a diminutive, little creature, handle these two big men if she had to.

"This man wouldn't stand during the anthem," said the veteran before Caper could say anything, "and tried to pull me down too. But I got to my feet. Look at him still sitting there. Look at that smirk on his face."

"That's a lie," shouted Caper, rising from his chair not realizing he had done so, not noticing any pain.

The people around them began jabbering. The security female spoke to a couple of them to find out what had happened here. They all confirmed to her the same thing. That man, and they pointed to Caper as that man, who was now standing, had remained seated the whole entire time the anthem was being sung.

"Come with me please," she told Caper.

"No, I will not. I didn't do anything wrong," he answered defiantly.

"That's your problem sir, you didn't do anything."

"I'm not going with you."

"Sir don't make me call for backup. You don't want me to do that now do you?"

Caper was starting to kind of enjoy this. He suddenly realized he was standing now. Not only standing physically but metaphorically standing for something, standing for his rights, the first time he had done so in years. A shot of adrenaline rushed through his body. It felt good and he harkened back to the days of his youth on campus.

"There's no law that says I have to stand during the anthem," he shrieked at her. This was his new lease on life, a new cause for him to espouse in his rusting years, a way to relive his glory days.

The security woman made the call. The game had started, and this fool needed to be hustled off the field as soon as possible. Two big men, not women, with muscles bulging out of their tight T-shirts, with ribbed abs also showing, were soon at her side. She took them aside and gave them the low-down on Caper. They began colluding as to what they were going to do with him and came to the obvious conclusion, remove him from the crowd. Then the two big guys got on each side of Caper and started hauling him away.

Now by this time Caper's two grandchildren were hysterical. What were these two big meanies doing to their grandpa they wondered? Emmie was crying and Noah was pacing back and forth frantically not knowing what to do. "Grandpa, Grandpa, don't leave us," shrieked Emmie as the big bad men hauled Caper out of sight. Caper was so mad he never felt his back pain. His hate for authority building inside him as he shouted out expletives at these thug

170

security men. They just ignored him, lifted him, and carried him away, his feet never touching the ground. The security woman tried to round up the two grandchildren, but it was like trying to round up a couple of stray cats. The kids ran from her panic stricken. Eventually she got one in each hand, with the communal help of the crowd, and told them not to worry that they'd be seeing their grandpa soon and they were going to meet some nice people now. The kids of course never heard any of this and they continued to resist crying, wailing pathetically the whole time she dragged them away.

None of this kerfuffle was caught by the network camera men, and women, televising the game. The league had an agreement with the networks that no protesting of any kind was to be broadcast for they feared the negative effects this may have on their tv ratings. This was in writing in a contract between the League, the players' union, and the networks. So, it was never known to those of the outside world what had happened live here today.

But someone there knew. Someone from the 'drive through' media who saw what had taken place, saw the crying grandchildren being hauled away by the gestapo police of the establishment, saw the opportunity for a story, an anti-administration story, and knew how to milk it. Paula Periodista, news hawkette, started typing her story on her laptop. She always carried it with her wherever she went because she never knew when a news story would break. And if one didn't break, well there was always a news story to make and fake and break out there somewhere. A story just waiting for her to snatch it up and make into news.

Meanwhile Caper had been taken to a room in the depths of the beast of the belly of the bowels of the stadium and kept there under lock and key in isolation as those in authority went about the business of 'trumping' up charges against him. They had exhausted all the traditional legal charges available that came to their conservative minds and now were invoking some new ones per the tweets of the President. They finally came to a consensus and read him the charges in a monotone voice. Caper got the traditional ones like disturbing the peace, disorderly conduct, public drunkenness, inciting a riot, etc. etec. but after that he wasn't familiar with any on the laundry list of new and improved politically charged charges against him. Caper did not keep up on current events anymore for he had no interest in them. They were just too boring to him. He was a low information voter. Besides they were the same old things he had lived through for years. Nothing ever changed. There was always some kind of hyped-up hysteria over this and that, that and this, over and over again, and now today everything little thing was made into something politically controversial big again, world without end.

Some woman read Caper his rights and recited the mantra that whatever he said can and would be used against him in a P. C. court of law. The faceless reader and reciter of his rights then asked Caper if he understood those rights.

But Caper did not answer yes or no. In fact, he said nothing and didn't even look at the woman officer. She didn't like that. The stereotyped officer, clean cut short butch haircut officer, then asked him this a second time if he understood his rights and again Caper said nothing still refusing to even acknowledge that the officer had spoken to him. She didn't like his attitude and after the third time this routine was repeated, she wrote up a bunch of new charges against Caper, which included among other things refusing to cooperate with law enforcement, disrespect to a law officer, and wasting an officer's valuable time, and much

much more. Caper again never answered when asked if he understood his rights as to these new charges. He had remained silent this whole time because either way, whether he answered yes or no, he knew his answer would be used against him. A yes or no could be used against him in an innumerable number of ways and means just like a congressional committee uses answers given them. Besides if one had a right to remain silent, to Caper's way of thinking anyway, it didn't make any sense to answer for one wouldn't be remaining silent then, would one. To Caper the right to remain silent meant the right not to answer, to say absolutely nothing. He had learned that in his college protest days when he refused to give the 'pigs' his name and address causing them a lot of time and inconvenience trying to figure out who in the hell they had just arrested. For he carried no id on him when he protested back then for that very reason.

All that was of course to no avail now as the pigs found out who he was, where he lived, what he did for a living, what he had for breakfast that morning, etc. etc. They took his wallet from him, got out his driver's license, and googled him. They found out more about Caper Kallenbach that day than Caper Kallenbach even knew about himself.

Now as to his grandchildren while all this was going on, well Paula Periodista was working on that. Working on it so hard that she was sure he would win a journalist prize for her 'journalistic' efforts. Already her headlines read: "Children forcibly separated from their grandfather by the President." It was a call to arms story that was answered by a nameless community organizer social worker, a woman social worker, male social workers were never allowed to work with small children, who took the children under her motherly hen wings. She got her organization's plethora of lawyers to file a suit against the Administration demanding the children be united with their parents immediately, stating a crime against humanity was willfully being evilly perpetrated by the federal government.

Noah and Emmie's parents were on vacation in, of all places in Mexico, as explained to them by Noah as he went on to relate to the authorities that they were staying with their grandfather for the week until their folks got back. But the community organizers couldn't release the children to a grandfather now in the county jail and since there was no one the children could be released to, the court, at an emergency hearing the following Monday, it was Monday because the football game was on Sunday, decided to leave the children in the custody of the state, the community social worker. That was fine with Paula for it kept her story, and her cause, get the President, alive and well and she could then milk it some more for all it was worth.

And so, she did. Outside the courthouse that day her photographer got an ever so heartbreaking, gut-wrenching picture of the children being led away, while they cried, by some big husky deputies, capturing all the children's fright, anguish, and grief. She was sure she was going to win the Pulitzer Prize for this.

More likely she'd win the Poultryzer Prize for such a chicken 's' story. The Poultryzer was a journalistic award created by the President per his Executive Order number something or other, that was awarded by him to the best chicken 's' story of the year by the drive through media. The letter 's' being known to all.

Caper was brought before a judge that Monday too, and at the insistence of the Prosecutor, one Mile Moles, a scrunched up squinty eyed little runt of a man, with beady pink eyes, requested bond be set at one million smackeroos. The reason for this he explained to Judge Trudith, Judge Trudith had been assigned this case at the request of Mr.

Mole because of her right-wing political agenda and was commercially known as Judge Trudy. Mr. Mole argued that Mr. Kallenbach was a danger to society in that if released he would incite others to disrespect the flag and thus cause protests, marches, and riots, both for him and against him, which the law enforcement forces of this great city of ours, would be unable to handle on such short notice. He then went on to cite some ancient history example facts of this occurring in 1968. Judge Trudy bought it for as said she was a no nonsense American and to her nonsense was best confined to a jail cell.

Judge Trudy agreed that this was a reasonable amount and bond was set as such. Caper had kept quiet the whole time and didn't answer any questions whether from Miles Mole or from Judge Trudy. He did this again because he knew that if he did speak, no matter what he said, it would be twisted into something, whether by the prosecution or the press, and used against him. He never told his reasoning on keeping quiet to Judge Trudy when she insisted, he answer because he thought certainly a judge would know this. But she didn't. Judy Trudy was starting to get mad at Caper for not answering her and was about to lose it. Her reputation, or rather it was her schtick on her tv show, was to lose it when she didn't like someone, and she was beginning not to like Caper a lot. But this was a high publicity real case and a tv case and she pulled herself together and got herself under control. She was under the microscope of the left-wing world of legal lunacy and would be damned if she gave them a bone to feed on. So, she decided to appoint an attorney for Caper. She assumed that he could afford one, but since he refused to fill out an affidavit as to his income and assets, to see if he could afford an attorney or not, and who can, she felt it best to avoid any more hassle or controversy than necessary and appoint someone for him. That was her plan anyway.

But the best laid plans of mice and women sometimes go astray like they did this day. F. Lee Dailey, attorney and counselor at law, foiled Judge Trudy's plans. F., the F was for Female she had told the public years ago at the start of her controversial legal career, Lee Dailey was a former ACLU attorney, volunteering her services to anyone she deemed worthy of and in need of her, provided they were left of center. So now today she had decided to come to the rescue of one Caper Kallenbach who had to be left of center because after all he refused to stand for the anthem, stand for the flag. One can not get more leftist than that she thought.

The local bar members called her Flea Dailey combining the F with Lee into one name Flee and then morphing it into Flea like the parasite. For that is what they thought of her, a parasite feeding her career off the downtrodden of society.

"I will be representing the Defendant Your Honor," she hollered as she ran up to the bench, out of breath and late as usual in her dark blue pants suit uniform.

Judge Trudy didn't care that much for F. Lee Dailey, but her intervention here spared her the decision of having to appoint someone to represent the defendant. This way she would not get blamed for appointing some inefficient ineffective counsel if things came to an appeal, which they always did.

"File your appearance of record then," ordered Judge Trudy.

"Here Your Honor is your copy," said Lee and handed the judge a copy, "And here's yours Miles," she said, handing Mr. Prosecutor a copy. 'I apologize for being late but I was," and here she went into some elaborate story about how she was saving someone else from a terrible injustice by the system, when Judge Trudy suddenly cut her off with a sharp, "spare us counselor."

"Yes, Your Honor," said Lee. "Now as to the matter of bail Your Honor. I believe it is excessive for the reason that," and here Judge Trudy cut her off again before she began her grocery list of reasons.

"Bail has already been set counselor. Call the next case Bailiff."

"But."

"But get your scrawny butt out of here, Counselor. That matter has already been decided," said Judge Trudy, having lost it now. Judge Trudy did not like Lee with a vengeance because she always dared challenge her. She believed Lee gave women lawyers a bad name.

That was true attorney Lee did have a scrawny butt just like Miles Mole did and she kind of even looked like him too with a scrunched-up hatchet face with a jutting jaw and beady dark, instead of pink, little squinty eyes. Though they were opposite sides of the judicial coin here today, either attorney could have passed for the other from a distance, and the only way to tell them apart was that Lee wore a blue suit and Miles a gray one, but he did have on a red tie though and a white shirt.

Mr. Mole was true to his name in that he had a tunnel vision view of justice. As to Lee she had a remora vision view of justice and fed off the great white shark of justice in the typical symbiotic relationship. Justice needed Lee too in order to justify its existence for without the bad, the triumvirate of the good, back, and ugly of justice could not survive. Lee had to protect her image as a championess of justice as well and feed off it. For this case was her next fix, her next rush to judgment.

177

Female Lee Dailey left the courtroom but not without having informed her client that she would come see him at the jail and discuss 'their' case tomorrow.

Meanwhile as to the two darling grandchildren, Noah and Emmie, they had been placed in a run down, underfunded, orphanage in an underprivileged neighborhood, and would remain there until they're parents got back from Mexico and could reclaim them. Of course, their parents would have to prove to the authorities that they were in fact their parents and not some sexual deviate child abusers come to steal the children. Their parents had been contacted by the U.S. authorities to come home and get their children. But they said that they couldn't possibly be back until a week from next Tuesday because that's when their plane tickets were for and they couldn't, actually didn't want to go to the trouble of getting them changed to anything sooner. The real reason though was that they had already paid for their vacation in advance and didn't want to cut it short and not get their money's worth. They were enjoying themselves immensely, having a high old time, away from the kids for a week, and certainly didn't want to get home to those two little hellions any sooner than necessary. Like all kids their kids behaved for Grandpa, but they raised holy hell at home for their parents. They needed this vacation to keep them from going bananas.

The Administration of Justice, a federal agency created by a recent Executive Order, and covering all aspects of justice whatever or wherever justice needed to be covered, the next day intervened in the matter of the legal custody of the grandchildren and got themselves appointed the children's legal guardian now instead of the state. Their attorneys had argued that their agency was needed here to administer justice because it was a federal issue now since the parents were in Mexico and thus nations were involved in international relations, and it might be that illegal aliens were trying to get into the country by using their children as a ploy. Judge Whackner, the judge assigned to the children's case, again at Mr. Mole's request, agreed and made a federal case of it.

Paula Periodista immediately picked up on all that federal case business and once again could not let this crisis go to waste. She hurried her, and it wasn't a scrawny little butt, but kind of a cute little butt, pell mell over to the orphanage with all her crew and their equipment. They marched in military style, began logistically setting up their mass weapons of the press, that is the most recent high-tech state of the art camera and recording devices, including drones, and began their assault on the truth. There she had the children pose, clutching their little fingers through the rusty chain linked fence with a look of pitiful desperation on their mournful cute little faces, squishing those faces against the wire, while staring blankly into the forbidden freedom beyond. Then she took an eye dropper and placed a few drops of water under each child's eyes and began her live report.

"We are gathered here today live at this riverhead fountain of injustice," she began waxing ever so poetically, ever so melodramatically, the cameras rolling, "That continues to flow from this administration." It wasn't actually live, though she had led the crowd they had bussed in there to believe that it was. She would take the film back to the station and they would edit it to fit their agenda before airing this dirty laundry in public three times on their newscasts today and a couple of times next week as well. "Where these two poor innocent little children are but the latest victims, in a string of victims, in this administration's war on families." Paula knew that a war on anything was the only way to go in the world today to get sympathy for her cause.

The cameras then got a close up of the children's tears but Paula didn't think it showed enough tears, so they did three retakes until she got the scene the way she wanted it and continued.

"Where these children, pawns of the administration, are being held captive at this Auschwitz style concentration camp that dares call itself an orphanage."

Paula continued on following the pre-written script her boss had given her and after a few more retakes she was satisfied with the results. But when she got to the end she didn't stick to the script. She took it upon herself to ad lib believing that her boss would be pleased with her for doing so and she could earn herself some brownie points. So, she ended with. "Mr. President," she said this ever so dramatically, "Tear down this fence. Let these children go. Let these children go." She actually didn't say these last two sentences. She kind of sang them.

"That's a wrap boys and girls," she shouted to her crew, and they all scurried away back and disappeared in the holes of their offices like the rats they were.

The next day Lee Dailey conferred with her client at the county jail. Caper's first concern was that his grandchildren were alright, and he asked about them before Ms. Dailey could say anything. She assured him that they were fine and that their parents would be home soon to retrieve them. Though as far as she was concerned, the longer the kids remained cooped up, the better it was in the court of world opinion for her since child imprisonment generated sympathy for her client that had a reading off the Richter scale of injustice and likewise for more hatred for the President. Once she got Caper calmed down, she began by reading the charges brought against him. At no time did she say why she volunteered as Caper's attorney. She did not expect him to ask why. She just assumed that he would be more than glad to have her represent him because of her reputation and that she was free. She didn't care about getting paid. It was the legal adrenaline high that she got from representing all these deranged, demented people with psychological problems that made her feel good about herself. She felt good when she could champion a cause not a client. It gave her a warm, fuzzy, glowing, tingly, feeling inside, a shot in the arm to her ego. Besides this case was sure to generate other paying clients in the future. Time is and always has been a lawyer's stock in trade as attorney A. Lincoln once said. And here her time was future money in the bank.

Caper didn't object to her representing him for the very reason that she was free. He had become conservatively fiscal in his old age, or in other words niggardly, and that word doesn't mean anything racial, look it up, to the point of ridiculousness. So, he was glad for the free legal services and sat there and patiently listened as she read off the list of charges. Again, he understood what disturbing the peace was, obstructing justice, disorderly conduct, public drunkenness, though he wasn't drunk, he never even got to finish his beer before they hauled him away, and the other generic common law crimes that she had recited but when that was over she stopped and said, "Now as to the violations, excuse me alleged violations, of an Executive Order,"

"A what?" interrupted Caper.

"An Executive Order."

"An Executive order, what the hell is that?" Caper didn't keep up on politics in his old age. He had had enough of that in his youth to last him a lifetime.

"That's when the President makes laws and orders for you to do or not to do something."

Though Caper was somewhat ignorant as to the workings of his government he thought back to what he had learned a lifetime ago in civics class in high school about the three branches of government, the legislative, the executive, and the judicial.

"Wait a minute," he interrupted. "If I remember right from civics class in high school that only the legislative branch can make laws, not the executive branch. How can that be?"

"The executive branch can make law now, well actually they've been doing it for years, by executive order because the legislature has delegated its legislative duty to the executive branch."

"Why?"

"Well, this way the legislators don't have to make any decisions, pass any laws that is, that puts them at risk at election time. Plus, as an added bonus, if they don't like an Executive order, and it's unpopular, they can attack it at election time to get votes."

"Unbelievable," said the politically ignorant Caper. "I didn't know the President had so much power. I bet he likes that."

"You bet he does," replied Lee, "because this way he can advance his agenda without having to go to all the trouble of passing a law. It's such a hassle passing a law nowadays you know, making deals, payoffs, compromises, stuff like that. It's time consuming, everybody's ego has to be fed, and it's costly. Executive orders are a win-win for both branches of government and for both political parties. By the way, what is civics?"

Little did Attorney Dailey know that there had once been a required high school course called civics that taught

students how the government in this great country of ours worked, worked on
paper anyway. It had been extinct for years not by an executive order but by the Department of Education as a non-essential course and thus those school districts who taught it would be denied federal funding if they did so. Its shelf life soon expired. Caper explained it to her best he could, but Lee was nonplussed by it all and to her it seemed like Caper was explaining rocket science something totally incomprehensible to her and the masses, kind of like politics was to Caper.

"Now," she said, "moving right along there are a dozen or so charges here as to violating the President's Executive Order as to Patriotism. I can read them all if you wish but they all say the same thing over and over again. The President likes to repeat himself, you know, likes to hear himself talk. I can sum them up if you wish or read them all to you."

"Sum them up please" replied the ever so polite Caper for he knew, just from being an old man, that everything a politician said could be boiled down to a few lines that stuck it to you the citizen one way or the other, no matter how much the politicians tried to spin it for themselves.

"Basically it says," and here Lee paused and for effect held the charges before her in both hands, arms extended as she wrinkled the paper noisily, and read from it as if it was a royal proclamation or edict, which it was, "that each person in attendance at a sporting event shall rise, stand, and remain standing at attention when the national anthem or any other patriotic song, the definition of a patriotic song to be later defined by further Executive Order, is playing until that song is completely over. However, if a fly over is performed at this event, then the citizen shall remain standing at attention until the fly over is completed. That's it in a nutshell from the hard nut to crack man himself our Royal Highness His Excellency the El Presidente."

That Attorney Female Lee Dailey's hatred for the President was venomous and this trial was her chance to take him down and was obvious to the world. She had been a left-wing looney from the day she applied for Law School where she took advantage of the looniness of the day then sweeping across academia nut land by claiming she was of Polynesian descent. It sounded better, more exotic, than Native American descent, and more minority-like when applying for a minority person's scholarship opening and she knew one was available for a Polynesian. Those on the admittance board knew she was obviously not of Polynesian descent just by looking at her blonde hair and blue eyes but because she was the only Polynesian applicant that had applied and they had one spot reserved for Polynesians only, and they were desperate for a Polynesian for diversity as required by federal law, that they said, "Forget it. It's Polynesian town," and they let her in.

"What are the penalties for violating this so-called Executive Order?" asked Caper.

"Well, those haven't been decided yet," Lee informed him, "but the President and his specially self-appointed advisory congressional committee staff are working on them. Scuttlebut is he's waiting for your trial to be over, see which way things flop in the political world, before he decides what punishment to invoke. This of course depends on the mood of the country then, but rest assured he'll give Judge Trudy little room in imposing her sentence."

"In other words, I'm doomed," said Caper as he slumped in his chair, his chin on his chest, his eyes fixed on the dirty floor of his jail cell contemplating the inevitable that awaited him.

But Lee always tried to see the good side of things.

"Well you could say, that from the sunny side of the street that is, is that you make hay while the sun shines and there's a harvest of hay, politically and socially agendized hay, to be made here," said Lee with a gleam in her eye, her head held high, and enthusiasm bubbling over in her voice conveying her crusading message that she was ready to take on the challenge of defying the system, the system that had done Caper, and countless others wrong countless wrongs.

Something in that farmersque reference in that speech of hers struck a patriotic chord in Caper's heart. For after all farmers had always been the true patriots of this great country of ours, acting as minutemen, bearing arms forever after as a well-regulated militia necessary to the security of a free State. In fact, Caper could almost hear Yankee Doodle being played in the background as she spoke.

'Just ask Oliver Douglas Holmes if you don't believe me," said Lee. "A judicial plethora of a cornucopia of socio-political harvest awaits us."

Caper didn't know what that meant, and he ignored it. Instead, he started to harken back to his days on campus again and how he had risen up against a President in defense of freedom back then, risen up against a President who wanted to take his freedom from him and use him as cannon fodder in the war against communism, and how he had lost that battle by being drafted. He was an old man now but something inside him had sparked, lit a fire in him, and once again his dipstick read half full not half empty. Now he wanted to relive his glory days before he kicked the bucket list. So, he decided that he was going to go down in the flames of glory, that he was going to be a suicide bomber in the never ending battle for truth, justice, and the American way.

But he didn't know how to go about all this and though he had been a liberal in his youth, old age had transformed him, without him even knowing it, into a conservative. He was a tottering old fool on the tottering edge of a split personality now. He decided he'd think on this for a while, before he acted, for he was not sure on which side of the horns of his dilemma he would fall from or be pushed from.

"What do you say we make a political circus out of all this since you're doomed anyway Caper. Go down in a blaze of glory," said Lee reading his mind, picking up on that faraway look in Caper's eyes. "It's been done before right here in Chicago before you know. We got us a Nazi judge here again and you can be the Chicago One instead of the Chicago Eight or Seven or whatever is was. What do you say to that Caper?"

"Does that mean I'd have to give up my right to silence?" he asked for he had prided himself on invoking his right to silence. Prided himself that he invoked it without an attorney having to tell him to do so.

"No, you don't have to give it up. Invoke it when it's to your advantage and tell it like it is, to use an ancient maxim, when it's to your advantage. Mix it up like that. Invoke it here. Don't invoke it there. That'll drive Judge Trudy bananas. Tell me why you are so insistent on your right to silence anyway?"

Caper went on to explain his theory for not answering to 'Do you understand your rights?'

"You know that's brilliant, Caper. I'm going to write that down," said Lee and she took out her legal pad and started writing. "I'm going to advise my clients to do that. You know you should have been a lawyer Caper. You seem to come by it naturally."

Upon hearing that Caper perked up even more, sat up straight, and a smile came across his face. Maybe he didn't need this woman after all. Maybe it's best that he represented himself. Maybe she wouldn't let him say what he wanted to say. He was still tottering, dithering again, on the edge of another dilemma now.

Lee knew what he was thinking. She could read his mind because at some point or other all clients thought they were lawyers and wanted to represent themselves. She couldn't let that happen here. This was her case, not his, her chance of a lifetime, not his.

"But" she said, coming to her own rescue, "It's best that I run the show here for there's a time to keep quiet and a time to sow the seeds of freedom by opening one's mouth and letting it all spout out in a waterfall of cascading wonderful words. Yet there's also a time to clam up and swallow the bitter pill of silence and only an attorney can know those times, not a client. Trust me in this Caper for I know those times. For we live in terrible times now and only an attorney can guide one through them. Trust me."

She was waxing way too poetic for a former factory union worker like Caper but on the other hand he gleaned some truth from what she had just said. On the other hand, the truth of the matter was Caper wanted to talk now. His attorney's advice be damned. He wanted to tell the world to stuff it, to put it politely, and he realized now in his old age that this would be his one last chance to do so. He was going to go for it, going to make a speech in court, but not tell her. So, he just nodded his head in approval.

"Now why didn't you stand anyway?" she asked him as if it was somehow important to this case.

He knew the real reason was because his back had been bothering him something terrible that day, but he didn't want to tell her that. There was no glory in that. The truth was just too boring here for this case, too mundane, too pedestrian. In fact, the truth might just set him free, and he didn't want to be set free by a medical defense like the defense of insanity was a medical defense that set people free. He wanted a trial, his day in court, now, today. He wanted martyrdom. So, he finally decided once and for all to go down as a suicide bomber for the left-wing liberals, which he had once been, who were so desperately fighting the Administration every waking hour of the day. The melting pot of liberalism had come to a boil in that senile brain of his brain and was about to erupt in a lava flow of wonderful words.

But then again, he still had his doubts. As said this actually went against the grain for him now because of his old age and he had actually come full circle and had come to like the President and what he stood for. He couldn't help this. He figured that was because our brains are just programmed that way, liberal in youth, conservative when old. He knew now that he would have to overcome his preprogrammed life somehow if he was going to do this.

"Well?" repeated Lee. She could see Caper was paying her no attention lost in thought. "Why didn't you stand up?"

Caper snapped out of it.

"I didn't stand because," and then Caper stopped. He didn't have any disrespect for the flag and didn't know what to say. "I don't know what to say," he said, so confused was he now, fearful that he would say the wrong thing to her that she didn't want to hear and stop him from testifying as to it.

"Don't worry about what to say," said Lee, coming to his rescue. "I'll tell you what to say. I'll write it all down for you what to say, go over it with you and explain it all to you what to say, and you can memorize what to say. How's that?"

Caper realized now that maybe this was best. He had morphed into a dithering nervous wreck and wanted this all over. The sooner the better. So he said, 'That's a good idea. I would appreciate that." Things had just become way too complicated for him to deal with all this political hogwash. Too deep for him and his limited brain power to process. Let the attorney handle it. He gave up his suicide bomber plan.

"Good it's settled then," replied Lee. "Look, I gotta run now. You're not the only one in the world that's been arrested, you know. I got other government systematically oppressed clients too that need my help."

F. Lee Dailey, attorney at law got up, shook Caper's hand, and hollered for the jailer to come get her. "Oh, by the way," she said to Caper, "we're not going to post bail, not because of the amount. I could get some rich multi-millionaire sympathetic psycho to our cause to do so, but that would be counterproductive because it's in your best interests to rot in jail, so to speak that is. The press loves to have people rot in horrible horrendous jail cells. It draws sympathy to their and our cause."

The jailer arrived, let Lee out, and Caper flopped down on his cot of a bed, put his hands behind his head and whimsically, now that he felt a little better and was encouraged some by his attorney's wonderful way with words, began humming 'Nobody knows the trouble I've seen.' Lee heard that and hollered back, "Keep it up. Oh yeah, by the way, see if you can get yourself thrown in solitaire. It'll help our case."

Though Caper acted up the next two days trying to earn a solo spot in solitary confinement, Prosecutor Mile Moles had instructed the sheriff's office not to let him do that, not to let him make a martyr of himself. Like good minion soldiers, the jailers followed orders.

In the meantime, as Caper languished in jail, numerous legal mumbo jumbo things, like motions to quash, motions to produce, discovery requests, etc. etc. ad nauseum were filed by Lee with the court about his upcoming trial. She filed them even though she knew she would lose, lose on all of them, which she did, but she did so because if she didn't, she could be charged with malpractice. Caper understood none of these 'legal' things. So, she explained everything to him, best she could anyway, to cover her butt again, to avoid the label of inefficient, ineffective legal counsel, which was grounds for appeal if she lost, and grounds for a malpractice suit too.

In the meantime, Caper's grandchildren were released from the children confinement center into the open arms of their loving parents. This took some time as the government kept asking Judge Whackner for more time to do bureaucratic endless paperwork that was absolutely necessary, or so they informed him. Judge Whackner kept granting them extensions for them to get their legal act together for he didn't want to make a mistake by denying them this and be overturned on appeal. He like all judges feared being overturned on appeal since it might make him look like an incompetent legal doofus and hurt them at reelection time.

When the children were released Paula Periodista and Company were there with bells on. She was prepared to play the 'children card' for the umpteenth time. It was her trump card. So she got the parents to pose for the camera outside of the compound, fingers laced through the chain link fence, their faces smushed against it, looking in soulfully, sorrowfully, sad as they anxiously awaited the release of their ever so precious children. She instructed them how to look soulfully, sorrowfully, sad, and anxiously, and after a couple of takes the parents got it done to Paula's satisfaction. The children were brought forth by two big, hired gun actors in rented prison guard suits, to a tearful but ever so heartwarming and joyful reunion with their aggrieved parents. It was a stellar performance to say the least and Paula stuck to the script and recited her lines flawlessly. In fact, she was so good in her role that she was later nominated for best performance by a news actress in a dramatic series by some kind or other of news organization mutual admiration society. She didn't win though. She protested and claimed that was because she wasn't a trans sexual enough of a minority person, LBG gay or whatever those folks called themselves she said, to be allowed to win. That statement cost her her job. She became a real estate agent after that, where one didn't have to be so honest, selling overpriced houses to people that really couldn't afford them causing the real estate bubble to burst again and a crisis that only congress could fix again with a mortgage industry bailout again.

Now as the trial date was fast approaching, Female Lee Dailey planned her strategy and told Caper what it would be. "We are going to attack the system," she said. "The system that done you wrong."

What else is new thought Caper.

"The system that has systematically oppressed you and countless others of you over millennials of time," she continued. She meant millennium but had Freudian slipped and fallen over that word. "Look you went to a football game right, and the players there were protesting right, and you were a former protester right, and thus you decided to join in sympathy with them protesting against the systematic racist oppression policies of this administration, right?"

Caper knew that she was only partially right, but he said "right" anyway.

"So, we have to rally behind the downtrodden, the aggrieved, and fight the good fight now like the football players are doing, don't we?"

Caper didn't think a professional football player making millions of dollars a year was exactly downtrodden or had anything to be aggrieved about but he answered "right" again because he knew that was the answer she wanted to hear and after all she was the attorney and she knew the law here not him and he had finally decided to put his life in her hands, sleazy as though they may be.

"We're going to play the race card here," she informed him, "because no one, not even the president, can trump the race card. The deck has been stacked against us so that the house always wins but oh no not this time. We'll show this country that the President is not playing with a full deck."

Caper was having trouble following that piece of card spiel legal logic but didn't want to appear dumb by asking any questions, so he let it go. The way he looked at all this was even if he didn't have a bad back, he still had a right to sit there and not stand when the anthem was being played. No one should deny him that right. It all boiled down to that as far as he was concerned.

So, the trial began. It was a pay for view television event for after all it was like a championship boxing match and a money-making event and no money-making event in America should never go to waste now should it. Ringside, or courtside, even though it wasn't a basketball kind of courtside, tickets were scalped at record setting prices. All proceeds from sale of courtroom seats and concessions, including the sale of beer, and the television rights went into the county coffers so county officials could give themselves a bonus at the end of this coming fiscal year.

Since the trial was being televised live, there were time restraints. The trial had to fit into a two-hour maximum time slot. Judge Trudy was already familiar with television court. She had her own, though it wasn't live, it was taped and then edited, courtroom drama show entitled: Kick Butt Justice, wherein, or so the public was led to believe it was real, real justice. The cases had actually been written by script writers and the suer and the suee were actors. It was a comedy show. The script always had Judge Trudy insulting the participants a la Don Rickles style. The masses ate it up. Why the show's producers and or the network weren't called out on this was the $64,000 question. Anyway, Judge Trudy would keep things under control here and confine the proceedings within the allotted time. But there would be no script here. She'd have to ad lib by doing her usual schtick.

"Call your first witness Mr. Mole," shrieked Judge Trudy in her raucous crow-like cawing voice.

"The State calls Caper Kallenbach," squeaked Mr. Mole.

Caper Kallenbach rose slowly. It was an effort for him to do so. He was still in pain, his back still bothering him, as he walked to the stand the pain visible on his face. He had been sworn before the show started, no sense wasting time broadcasting a boring swearing in ritual everyone out there already knew about. Attorney Dailey had agreed to let Mr. Mole call her client first in the matter of time efficiency and that she wanted him crucified as soon as possible to play upon the sympathies of the national TV audience at home.

Mr. Mole was well prepared. He carried with him his soap box and placed it next to Caper who was sitting in the elevated witness chair. He climbed up on it, wrinkled his nose, and took out a fist full of papers from his inside vest pocket. He looked Caper in the eyes, best he could anyway, and began.

"Mr. Kallenbach I have here," and he waved the papers clutched in his right hand at the defendant, "the bad and the ugly about you. Your college arrest records" He paused for dramatic effect and turned to the camera and gave it his most judicially stern look. "You were arrested back in the day for protesting the war, weren't you?"

"Well, ya, but." But before Caper could say another word Mr. Mole cut him off.

"You were a hippie back then, weren't you?"

"Well, ya, but."

"And you're still a hippie today aren't you or you wouldn't be wearing your hair in a ponytail like you're doing now, would you?"

"Ya, but."

"And you think you can fool this court, no fool America, by coming here in a suit and tie don't ya? You think you can fool everyone into thinking that you're just an average everyday down to earth type of good guy, don't you? But you can't fool the public now can you Mr. Kallenbach because the stripes on a cheetah can't be changed now, can they?" Mr. Mole had gotten so carried away with himself with that last entourage of bombarding words that he had rattled them off so quickly nonstop, like a runaway train, without really thinking about what he was saying, kind of like this sentence is doing, that he didn't pick up on the sniggles coming from the courtroom crowd for his faux paw about cheetahs. And he never gave Caper a chance to 'Ya but' answer and continued.

"You didn't stand for the anthem because you're in sympathy with all those ridiculously tattooed football players, aren't you?" Mr. Mole knew from the polls that his office had conducted that the public was losing sympathy for the football players and starting to think of them as a bunch of spoiled little kids throwing a fit, trying to get attention, and furthermore that the public didn't care for all that overtattoing.

"No, I'm not in sympathy with any tattooed," and here Caper made the air quotation marks as he said the word tattooed, "football players," he said, mocking Mr. Mole.

Lee rose from her chair upon hearing Caper say that. He wasn't supposed to say that.

"Objection Your Honor. The defendant is not sticking to our game plan."

That was a new one on Judge Trudy. She punted to Mr. Mole.

"Mr. Mole, what say you?"

"Tough noogies is what I say, Your Honor."

"Tough noogies it is then. Objection overruled. Continue Mr. Mole." From that day forward the phrase tough noogies became a legitimate legal lexicon phrase used in courtrooms all across America.

Mr. Mole saw his opening, took it, and blitzed, hoping to sack Caper for a legal loss.

"So, if you're not in sympathy with the ball players, then you're a lone wolf, a lone wolf terrorist, disrespecting the national anthem and our flag aren't you?"

Now that did it for Caper. Though he had decided not to make a suicide bomber of himself and do what his attorney thought best, well Mr. Mole had just pushed him over the edge that day. Caper Kallenbach couldn't take it anymore and went ballistic. Now was the time to rise. Go for it. For a man has to do what a man has to do at times like these. Women could do something different, but a man has to do what a man has to do. He dodged the blitz by veering to the right.

'First of all," he began, "I have no sympathy for people who put graffiti all over their bodies. It's disgusting. These people," and by people white people thought he meant black people, "think it's cool to gaudy up their bodies with a bunch of clever corny sayings and goofy disgusting pictures.

But it's stupid if you ask me. I tell you if God wanted us to have tattoos, God would have had us born with tattoos now, wouldn't He?" Caper stopped, paused for effect, played to the camera with a scowl on his face, and turned to the courtroom crowd and put on his best red, as in red blooded American, white, especially white, and blue, but not Democrat blue, patriotic face.

The crowd loved it. There were a number of fundamentalist evangelicals there and they appreciated invoking God into all this. They began buzzing and bobbing their heads mindlessly up and down in approval, like a bobble head dog on the dashboard of a Mexican American's car.

Lee picked up on all this. Her client's sympathy rating just went up six points. Time to change the game plan. Time to call an audible. She rose and spoke again.

"I withdraw my objection Your Honor."

"It's already been overruled, Counselor," squawked Judge Trudy.

"I still move to withdraw it Your Honor and have it stricken from the record."

Judge Trudy blew out a visible breath between her extended lips, flapping them audibly as she did so. The crowd ate it up.

"What say you Mr. Mole?" she said as she rolled her eyes.

"I object to her objection Your Honor on the grounds that two wrong objections don't make a right objection." He didn't know what that exactly meant but it sounded good like two wrongs don't make a right was in there somewhere.

"Objection to the objection overruled," ruled Judge Trudy.

The show's producer signaled Judge Trudy that it was time for a commercial.

"We'll take a recess now," announced Judge Trudy, "for a word from one of our sponsors, Legalroom dot com, and be right back," The cameras went off Judge Trudy and the commercial began airing. She noticed that the crowd was still buzzing talking favorably about Caper and that they were mainly old people, for after all who could afford the price of admission here but old retired well to do old people. And she also noted that without exception no one had a tattoo. Well at least no visible tattoos. Judge Trudy liked that. She didn't have one either, not a visible one that is.

The five minutes of commercials were over in five and a half minutes. The cameraman signaled for Judge Trudy to begin. She did.

"Continue Mr. Mole," she said.

Mr. Mole needed to shift the momentum back to the prosecution. Caper had become the crowd's sweetheart with that anti tatoo speech of his.

"So, you're not in sympathy with the football players protesting because they're African-Americans and you're a racist isn't that correct Mr. Kallenbach? Being a racist is another one of your many unAmerican activities, isn't it?" Always play the race card thought Mr. Mole. No one wants to be called a racist. No one can trump the race card.

"Look," answered Caper. "I don't give a rodent's rear end what any of those black dudes do. If they want to protest 'governmental systematic oppression of black people in America' that's their business, not mine." Caper air quoted again with his fingers the words 'governmental systematic oppression of black people in America. "I don't know why everybody's getting their knickers all in a twist about this anyway. Who the hell cares what these black dudes do? Why pay any attention at all to them? Hell, they been doing it for years, protesting. I even joined them back in the day, back in '72, when I was in college. Blacks protesting was a big thing then. Remember the Olympics. That's what they do, they protest. They did it then, they do it now, and they'll be doing it ad nauseam into the future. In fact, if you ask me, it's starting to get downright boring. Black people have been done to death. Besides all this not standing for the flag business, it's just another way for them to stick it to the man."

The courtroom crowd inhaled a collective gasp. Their eyes bugged out as they did so in disbelief as to what they had just heard. No one, no one in their right mind that is, would talk that way about black people. Mr. Mole smiled. Lee slumped in her seat her hand on her forehead. A headache was coming on.

"So, you don't care if these players don't stand for the anthem just like you didn't care to stand for the anthem? Isn't that correct? Is that your way of sticking it to the man too? The hippie way?" Mr. Mole had him on the ropes now.

"Yes, I don't care and nobody else should either. This whole flag thing is freaking ridiculous if you ask me. What's the point of getting all worked up about it anyway?"

"Your witness Ms Dailey," smirked Mr. Mole quitting while ahead. A good attorney always quits when he's ahead.

Lee was desperate. She had to get this back on track and now. Mr. Mole had sidetracked her playing the race card, making this a black and white issue, and she was going to have to pull his plug, show the television audience that her client was not a racist, and that he was in fact sympathetic with the plight of African Americans in America.

"But you do agree, don't you Caper that African Americans have been, and still are, systematically oppressed in this country of ours don't you?"

"No, not anymore."

Lee put both her hands to the sides of her head.

Caper was not going to be denied. "And I'll tell you why."

But Lee denied him, cut him off, and denied him his right to free speech before he could say another word.

"Objection to my client's answer Your Honor as being over responsive."

That was another new one for Judge Trudy, over responsive, so she deferred to Mr. Mole again, "What say you Mr. Mole?"

Mr. Mole knew that if Lee was claiming it was over responsive then he had to say it was under responsive, had to take the opposite side of an issue whether he wanted to or not, for that was his job.

"The issue here Your Honor is her client not being over responsive but her client being under responsive not responding to the President's call for all Americans to stand for the flag." Mr. Mole was proud of himself for that response, it was not over responsive or under responsive but a just right responsive, turning her objection around on her, putting her on the defensive.

"Your Honor," interjected Lee. She didn't know what to say next. She had only objected to shut her client up for sometimes clients slit their own throat by talking too much, over responding as she called it. Though she didn't have a legal reason to object, she continued anyway. She had to take the noose off her neck before she died on the vine. "It's not my client that's over-responsive," she countered. "It's the President that's over responsive to anything that affronts him, affronts us all. Over responsive by issuing Executive Orders and putting innocent citizens on trial for exercising their rights. One cannot overreact to an overreaction. In fact, it is one's duty to overreact to an overreaction."

Lee thought that sounded good but in her heart of hearts she knew it sounded confusing to the TV audience at home who sat there scratching their heads trying to determine if what she had said was brilliant or ridiculous or brilliantly ridiculous or ridiculously brilliant or any combination thereof.

Finally Judge Trudy said, "Objection overruled. The Defendant may answer. What did you wish to say Mr. Kallenbach?'

"I just wished to say Your Honor. That black people are no more systematically oppressed than any of us. The government can tax you, take your property, imprison you, and even take your life. We're all oppressed when they do these things to us. And though they can do all these things to us, they can never take away our rights as Americans unless we let them. And by God, as an American I'm not going to let them take mine. I'm going to protect my, no our, no all of ours, God given rights as Americans."

That did it. That swung the momentum back to Caper. God and America and rights did it. He was on a roll and Lee now was going to keep him rolling on.

"In fact, you already have protected those rights by serving in the army haven't you?"

Everyone's jaw dropped in the courtroom and with ten million viewers at home doing likewise.

"You served proudly in Vietnam, didn't you?"

"Well, I served."

Lee decided to quit right there before Caper self-imploded himself again. "Your witness Mr. Mole."

Mr. Mole went for the jugular and sunk his teeth into Caper's neck now on the chopping block of justice.

"So, you served but not proudly Mr. Kallenbach. Is that it?"

"Let's just say I served."

"Oh, you can't muddy up the waters on us like that now Mr. Kallenbach. Trying to make a molehill out of a mountain are you Mr. Kallenbach? Or are you trying to have us forget about that little caper of yours Caper where you tried to burn down the ROTC building on campus?" Mr. Mole was proud of himself for this little, and it was very little, play on words of the defendant's first and last name. But no one there picked up on it and Mr. Mole went down swinging.

"Your witness Ms. Dailey," said Miles Mole quitting while he was ahead again or not that too far behind depending on how one looked at it.

"Your Honor," said Caper. "I'd like to say something."

"Objection," hollered Lee rising from her chair.

"Objection overruled," squealed Judge Trudy. This ought to be good, she thought. She wanted to hear what Caper had to say. "The Defendant has a right to be heard Counselor. After all this trial's all about one's rights, the right to be heard, now, isn't it? Make your speech Mr. Kallenbach," Judge Trudy said warmly, invitingly, seducingly.

"Look Judge, all I want to say is that when you go to a ball game, you go to see a ball game. That's what you pay your money for. You don't pay your money to go to a political rally which is what ball games in this country have turned into today. Did you know that before World War I they never even played the national anthems at baseball games? It all came about because of war then to get the public patriotically all worked up back then and it continues today because of 911 and the war on terrorism. Now they've even added God Bless America too at baseball games during the seventh inning stretch. They don't sing Take Me Out to The Ballgame anymore like Harry Carey used to. It's gotten to the point of ridiculousness. If you want to sing at a ball game, then sing the team's fight song for God sakes. They all got one. Don't make a captive audience be forced to sing the anthem. That's something Kim So Dumm or whatever his name is over there in North Korea would do. That's something Stalin, Mao, and Hitler did. You know why not extend it to the start of everything like at a movie theater where there's a captive audience. Yah we should have done it at the start of this show. Big Brother, or should I say Big Person, is here people. It's time to resist, to stand up and fight the good fight."

That blew the lid off his now boiling over pot. Everyone got splattered and everyone didn't know whether to wipe it off or let it stick for there were those that liked and those that hated what Caper had just said. Lee made a halfhearted attempt to rise and object but was out of legal gas and slumped back down in her chair again. Mr. Mole burrowed himself in a legal book on his table making it look like he was looking for an answer buried in there somewhere.

Caper inwardly and outwardly smiled. He was proud of that speech. He got down from the witness stand.

"Hold on there," hollered Judge Trudy. "You're not done yet. Where do you think you're going?"

"I'm going to the people Your Honor. Taking my case to the people." And he went over and got Mr. Mole's soap box, picked it up, placed it directly in front of the camera for the TV audience at home and spoke. "I have not yet begun to fight." John Paul Jones would be proud. Caper continued.

"There's a few more things I'd like to mention here ladies and gentlemen," he announced as he got up on his soap box and straightened out his rumpled suit. "With your permission of course," he said politely, addressing the TV audience and not Judge Trudy.

"Please do. Please do," answered an unknown face in the crowd. That was enough of an invitation for Caper, not that he really needed one anyway, and he began.

Judge Trudy looked to the show's producer for guidance. It was clear to her that his signal was to let Caper run his mouth. Good drama. Good for a sequel and this would help hype it.

"First as to Mr. Mole making this a black, white issue, a race issue, it is not."

Caper said that even though he knew it was wrong. He knew race was the underlying current of all this for only black players did not rise, no white players knelt, when the anthem was played. This had been churning and roiling for some time now in the belly of America and this trial had brought it all foaming and bubbling to the surface regurgitated upward into the mainstream sewer of our discontent. Caper didn't care what the black players did, and he had to get the focus away from race since everything had become so racially oriented in this country.

So, he said, "It's about bullying." Bullying, everybody was against bullying. "Political correctness bullying, bullying whether it comes from the left correcting every sentence we say or from the right bullying us to stand for the anthem, it's all bullying just the same, all based on your own political agenda. It's all peer pressure. It's all some people trying to tell other people what to think, to say, and to do. It's all you know about America, and I won't say those two words here, since we're on TV, but I'm sure you know what I mean. So, let's do as they say in the ads on tv, let's end bullying, and I'll go further and say let's end political correctness, let's end political correctness bullying. I thank you."

Caper got off his soap box and went and sat down by his attorney. She had come back to life with that speech of his. She liked and approved of it. Couldn't have done it better herself. She would use it in her final argument to hit another home run just like Caper did.

And so, the crowd came to life, as they all rose from their seats as one, and began clapping and chanting USA, USA, some wiping tears from their eyes as they did so, giving Caper a standing ovation.

Judge Trudy was getting a signal now from the show's producer to wrap it up as he kept pointing to his watch. The producer was used to doing sitcoms and was well versed in managing showtimes and it was time to end the show on a high note.

"Okay counselors time for final arguments," announced Judge Trudy. "Mr. Mole, your turn."

"Thank you, Your Honor." Mr. Mole went and retrieved his soap box and set it, not to the left nor to the right, but in the center of the courtroom, and climbed up on it.

"Ladies and gentlemen of the TV viewing jury at home," he began looking into the camera.

Judge Trudy was not going to render a decision here today. No, the tv viewing public was. Those souls who had paid for the privilege of pay for view could now decide the fate of Mr. Caper Kallenbach by voting from the comfort of their own home. All they had to do was pay a slightly additional fee for the right to vote and then call in their verdict by either dialing 1-800-CONVICT or 1-800-ACQUIT. It was as simple as that, a truly American way of administering justice.

"Ladies and gentlemen," repeated Mr. Mole. "Caper Kallenbach is not the only one on trial here today. America herself is also on trial and you will do no finer greater service to this great again country of ours but to find America innocent and find one Caper Kallenbach guilty. The President, the commander in chief, has issued an order, and this good soldier Mr. Kallenbach, as he likes to think of himself for having served his country, has willfully refused to follow it. Soldiers follow orders. He didn't. In fact, he disobeyed an order. A soldier can be shot for not obeying a legal order. We are now engaged in yet another war against freedom. A war to destroy America as conducted and driven by the socialist left. Is it asking too much to counter this terrorism on our democracy for one to stand for the national anthem when it is being played? No! No, it is not asking too much to stand up for freedom, for the American men, and women, who have stood up for, and yes some even laid down their lives for? Now maybe if Mr. Kallenbach was in a wheelchair, we could excuse him or even if he had some kind of back problems and couldn't rise, we could excuse him, for we Americans are an understanding and sympathetic people. But that's not the case here. The case here is that we have an old hippie who's never grown up. An old hippie that's proud of himself for defying his country, then and now, and we cannot condone, no we cannot allow him and other un-Americans like him to do that. For to do so is to let chaos, anarchy, and yes, even worse, socialism run, rule, and ruin our lives and our country. The President's order is a reasonable, no it's a great order, and as such must be obeyed or surely this country will be on the road to hell in a handbasket. Vote Mr. Caper Kallenbach guilty and count on your President to issue an executive order as to what is fair, but still a painful punishment for violating a patriotic order. I'm sure you won't be disappointed. Trust in our leader, our fearless leader. I thank you."

"Ms. Dailey showtime," barked Judge Trudy. "Make it quick."

F. Lee Dailey went over, picked up Mr. Moles' soap box and flung it aside.

"People," she said, "you're not going to hear any corny speeches like that from me. From me you're going to hear the truth. Mr. Mole fumbled, fondled, bobbled, and couldn't handle the truth. But you can. The truth of the matter is that all this 'political correctness' whether it comes from the left wing loonie liberals or the right-wing wackos is bullying as my client said, plain and simple, peer pressure gone wild. Ya go to a ballgame to watch a ball game. Ya didn't go to be part of a political rally. If you wanted to do that you'd go to a political rally of the party of your choice, you'd go to a fourth of July parade or a Memorial Day service somewhere, not a ball game. That's the way it should be done. Not at a ballgame where they've got you trapped, where you're a captive enslaved audience. You don't want to stand up, but you're scared not to for fear of the society's disapproval, society's repercussions. Ball games are even getting worse now as my client said with flyovers and God Bless America. Where will it all end people? I'll tell you where it will end with Big Brother, or should I say Big Sister, or should I say Big Sibling to be perfectly politically correct, that's where it will end. And it won't end with just verbal abuse either. It will end with physical abuse of all those not 'politically correct.' It's only a step away. You don't have to be Nostradamus to see the brown shirts coming. You don't have to be Nostradamus to see that we are on the road to hell paved with the so-called good intentions of a President gone mad. Intentions that Mr. Mole so proudly proclaims are rooted in the name of patriotism but are really rooted in fascism. Time to stop caring America what some else thinks. Time to stop mind control no matter what side of the fence it comes from. Don't let political rhetoric control your mind, your life, for it will ruin both and your country. Don't let a President be a dictator and tell you what to do. Vote 1-800-ACQUIT. I thank you."

The crowd was awed by Lee's speech. They were bobbing their heads up and down affirmatively again. But the cameras never showed that. Time was up. The cameras zoomed in on Judge Trudy.

"Thank you, Counselors," she said. "That concludes this case. Time for you at home to cast your votes now," she said and then she recited the numbers again. Duh like the American People could not remember them because of their short attention spans or lack of brain power. But there was some truth to that. The broadcast then cut to a commercial for Judge Trudy's new show, Animal Court where real animals sue real animals, not people animals. The show was PETA approved because after all animals had the right to sue each other too just like real people do.

The pay for view viewers had up to midnight tonight to call in their vote. The results would be announced on PCNN the next morning even before their first 'Impeach the president. We got the goods on him this time,' breaking news' story of the day was to be aired like the dirty laundry it was.

But there was a problem, hacking. Whether it was foreign or domestic or right-wing whacko or left wing loonie could not be determined for there were far more votes counted than the number of people who had subscribed to pay for view in the first place. But the results did not matter anyway as far as the network was concerned, for the verdict was already a foregone conclusion. The tv executives had already declared Caper guilty before the show started. That way there would be a sequel for the sentencing hearing. Though Judy Trudy was not allowed to decide the case, the tv executives, per their own executive order, had decided to let her impose the sentence once the President set the parameters of punishment. The public would be demanding a Judge Trudy sentencing. Nothing else would do. In fact, they were counting on two sequels, the sentencing hearing and the appeal, for after all the trial had been such a huge financial success that they could not let the sequels go to waste now could they. America loves its courtroom dramas as evidenced by the number of shows already broadcast daily and this one was the topper on the tinseled-up Christmas tree of judicial broadcasting.

But there was a little problem, a catch forty-four, that's twice as bad as a catch twenty two, for the President didn't want to, for political reasons of course, issue his order until he knew the results of the voting and the broadcast company didn't want to declare Caper guilty until they knew what his punishment was to be. For if it just amounted to a slap on the wrist, there would be no sentencing hearing worth broadcasting and certainly no sequels to follow and they were banking on those things.

So ironically the President was at a Mexican standoff with the media and the media ironically was at an ethical standoff with itself, and neither knew how to deal with it, both wishing they could wash their hands of it somehow.

So, Mr. Caper Kallenbach languished in jail and died a slow death, not only there, but in the media too. He became the 'forgotten man' of the twenty first century political golddiggers and died an unceremonious death rotting in prison a few years later. He was given a military funeral though for it had been ordered by executive order, number something or other, that all those serving their country are mandated to be buried with full military honors and their family receive a flag. The grandchildren got the flag. They treasured it.

The term had come to its end now and the students were oh so glad for they had enough of all this ancient political bull nonsense. Political bull didn't exist anymore either and thus it was quite difficult for them to grasp, understand, and relate to the concept thereof. The discussion of Caper Kallenbach they deemed boring and stupid and no ne contributed much. They were all glad the course was over and wanted to get out of there. Professor Hillary picked up on this and dismissed the class early.

So, they all took the exam, regurgitated what the Professor Hillary wanted to hear, in other words her agenda, and they all passed. No one is allowed to fail nowadays. The reason being that it might upset the fragile little egos and psyches of today's youth if they did so. Today's students aren't programmed to deal with failure. Everyone has to be a winner. In fact, everyone gets nothing less than an A. Now Johnny's A might differ from Susie's A but they were still A's on their own respective scales of equitable grading. After all that was the whole point of a subjective essay exam to adjust each student's grade to each student's own individual ability. So therefore, it only logically followed that whatever the student wrote had to have been to the best of that particular student's own ability and thus that student deserved an A.

And thus, Professor Hillary so gave everyone an A and then immediately she went right back to burying herself in the ancient archives of history looking for something. Something that happened in those oh so troubled times of the early twenty first century. Something to vindicate her family name concerning an election back then. Back then in the days of knife to the hilt politics, the days of American political fairy tales.